THE BORGIA CABINET

THE BORGIA CABINET

J. S. FLETCHER

BROWNSTONE BOOKS

Originally published in 1932.

INTRODUCTION

Joseph Smith Fletcher (1863–1935) was an English journalist and author. He wrote more than 230 books on a wide variety of subjects, both fiction and non-fiction, and was one of the most prolific English writers of detective fiction—the work for which he is chiefly remembered today.

Fletcher was born in Halifax, West Yorkshire, the son of a clergyman. His father died when he was eight months old, and his grandmother took him in and raised him on a farm in Darrington, near Pontefract, in Yorkshire. He was educated at Silcoates School in Wakefield, and after some study of law, became a journalist at age 20.

He started work as a sub-editor in London, but soon returned to Yorkshire, where he worked first on the Leeds *Mercury* using the pseudonym "A Son of the Soil," and then as a special correspondent for the *Yorkshire Post.* Among other things, he covered Edward VII's coronation in 1902.

Fletcher's first books published were poetry. He then wrote numerous, and now largely forgotten, works of historical fiction and history, many dealing with Yorkshire. His regional work led to his selection as a fellow of the Royal Historical Society.

Michael Sadleir stated that Fletcher's historical novel, *When Charles I Was King* (1892), was his best work. Fletcher wrote several novels of rural life in imitation of Richard Jefferies, beginning with *The Wonderful Wapentake* (1894), but it wasn't until 1914, when Fletcher wrote his first detective novel, that he truly found his calling.

Over the last two decates of his life, he went on to write over a hundred more mysteries, many featuring the private investigator Ronald Camberwell.

Fletcher is sometimes incorrectly described as a "Golden Age of Detective Fiction" author, but he is in fact an almost exact contemporary of Arthur Conan Doyle, the creator of Sherlock Holmes. The bulk of his detective fiction works considerably pre-date the period considered the Golden Age, and even those few published within it do not conform to the closed form and strict rules professed, if not unfailingly observed, by Golden Age writers.

His work is still enjoyable today. Although some volumes have mildly racist elements, as were common in fiction of the era, the modern reader should keep in mind the period in which they were originally published.

—Karl Wurf
Rockville, Maryland

CHAPTER I
POISON!

A powerful automobile which dashed up to the front of Aldersyke Manor at precisely ten o'clock that June morning, after doing, as its driver proudly observed, the twenty-two miles' run from London in something less than record time, contained but one occupant, an alert-looking, sharp-eyed, smartly-dressed young man, who, as he advanced to the door, gave a swift glance all along the façade of the big house and was quick to notice that in every window the blinds and curtains were drawn. He knew from this that there was death in the house, and when a solemn-faced butler answered his ring at the bell he spoke in befitting accents.

"Superintendent Harding?" he asked, inquiringly. "I think he's expecting me here—Detective-Sergeant Charlesworth, from Scotland Yard."

The butler made no effort to conceal his surprise at the visitor's appearance and youthfulness—evidently his idea of a detective officer was of the old-fashioned sort. But as he looked his astonishment he stepped promptly aside, motioning Charlesworth to enter.

"This way, sir," he said, closing the door and turning into an inner hall, and from that to a corridor which apparently ran the length of the ground floor. "Mr. Harding told me to bring you straight to him—he's with the doctor."

Charlesworth made no remark: he had no idea at that moment as to the reason of his being sent down so hurriedly to this Hertfordshire country house. But as he followed his guide he kept his eyes open, and by looking about him and by occasional glances at the interiors of rooms the doors of which stood open as he passed, he gathered that this was the house of a very rich man—the furnishings, the pictures, the books, everything that he saw indicated wealth. Another thing struck him, too—there was nobody about in this big place; the corridor was empty save for himself and the butler, the rooms by which they walked were empty; there was a strange silence in the place. When his guide threw open a door and showed him into what was evidently a study or business room, and he saw two men talking there, he noted that their conversation was being carried on in subdued tones, as if, though they were closeted in strict privacy, they were afraid of even the walls around them.

Of these two men Charlesworth at once recognized in one, a tall, burly man in uniform, the local superintendent of police at whose urgent request he had been sent down from headquarters in such haste; the other was unmistakably a medical man. They turned as he entered; each followed the butler's example in showing some surprise at the newcomer's comparatively youthful appearance. But Charlesworth went straight to business as he made a formal bow to them.

"Good morning, gentlemen! Detective-Sergeant Charlesworth, from the Yard—at your service, Superintendent," he said. "Got down here as quickly as I could after receiving orders. May I ask what it's about?"

Harding looked at the doctor; the doctor nodded.

"What it's about," said Harding, "is just this. I don't know if you're aware of it, but this place, Aldersyke Manor, is the residence of Sir Charles Stanmore. Perhaps you've heard of him?—senior partner in the firm of Stanmore and Gilford, solicitors, Lincoln's Inn Fields, and quite apart from his practice a very wealthy man—very wealthy indeed, I'm told. Well, Sir Charles was found dead in his bed this morning, and, from an examination which Dr. Holmes has made of the body——"

"A preliminary examination," interrupted Holmes.

"Well, a preliminary examination," continued Harding. "Dr. Holmes thinks——" He checked himself, again looking at the doctor. "I suppose I'd better tell him, straight out?" he asked. "No use in concealing anything, now, eh, doctor?"

"No use at all!" said Holmes. "It's what he's come for."

"Well, Dr. Holmes thinks that he's strong grounds for believing that Sir Charles Stanmore died from the effects of poison," concluded Harding, with a wave of his hand. "That's it! And of course, it's got to be cleared up!"

Charlesworth turned on the doctor, eyeing him critically. He decided that Holmes was the sort of man who wouldn't give an opinion of any sort unless he had strong grounds for it.

"You really think he was poisoned, doctor?" he asked. "Well—might it have been self-administered? Suicide?"

"No grounds for that!" said Holmes. "Why should he take his life? He was a very wealthy man, only middle-aged, active, in good health, with everything to live for. I knew him well—he was the last man in the world to commit suicide."

"Then—somebody poisoned him? You think that?" suggested Charlesworth.

"I think he was poisoned. I think the autopsy which is absolutely necessary will establish that," replied Holmes. "The fact is, I am sure of it!"

Charlesworth dropped into a chair by the side of a big desk which stood in the centre of the room and pulled out a note-book and a pencil.

"Let me get a few facts, Superintendent," he said. "To start with, how old was Sir Charles?"

Harding reflected.

"I should say about fifty-five," he answered.

"Married?"

"Yes. He was married—first time, too—only three years ago. Lady Stanmore is, I should say, twenty years younger than her husband."

Holmes made a sound in his throat indicative of dissent.

"I'm afraid you're quite out there, Harding," he said, dryly. "Lady Stanmore is at least thirty years younger than her husband. She's not more than twenty-five now."

"That so?" said Harding. "Oh, well—I don't know her very well—only seen her two or three times. A lot younger, anyway."

Charlesworth was writing in his book. He looked up as his pencil ceased to move.

"Any children?"

"There have never been any children," replied Holmes.

"Get on together?" asked Charlesworth with apparent indifference.

"I think nothing is known to the contrary," said Holmes.

"Either of you seen Lady Stanmore this morning?" inquired Charlesworth.

"I have seen her," replied Holmes. "She is, of course, not fit to see anyone but a medical man at present."

"Friends with her?" asked Charlesworth.

"Her sister-in-law, Mrs. John Stanmore, is with her," said Holmes. "Fortunately, Mrs. John Stanmore is staying in the house."

"Before I go any further into matters," remarked Charlesworth, "I'd like to know if you're going to call in expert assistance about this poison theory, doctor. We must have an absolutely definite——"

"Yes!" said Holmes. "We've telephoned for Dr. Salmon, of the Home Office."

"The man, of course!" assented Charlesworth. "That's all right.

He'll come to your place, I suppose? Well, you'll let us—the Superintendent and myself—know the results of your examination and conference as soon as ever you can, won't you? And—if you're going now, doctor—just another question. I suppose you were well acquainted with Sir Charles as a local resident? Well, do you know if he had any enemies? Do you know of anybody who would wish him dead? Have you got any theory of your own—that you can suggest to me?"

"No!" replied Holmes, emphatically. "No! I can suggest nothing. All I can say is that I believe he was poisoned, and that the poison was not self-administered."

He made some remark to Harding about the necessary coroner's inquest, and went away, and Charlesworth, left alone with the Superintendent, turned on him.

"The beginnings of a mystery, eh, Superintendent?" he said. "Well, I'd better get to work on it. Between you and me, I'm keen on it. I'll tell you something. This is Case Number One with me!"

"What do you mean?" asked Harding.

"I mean," replied Charlesworth with a laugh, "that it's the first murder—if it is murder—case I've ever been put on to, that is, to work at as principal. And you can jolly well bet I'm going to make good at it! If Sir Charles Stanmore has been poisoned, that's murder, and I'm going to find out the murderer's identity. And now let me get to work. Can I have the use of this room?"

"I suppose, as we've been called in, we can have the run of the house," replied Harding. "What do you want to do—first?"

"First I want to see the man, or woman, or whoever it was, that found Sir Charles dead this morning," replied Charlesworth. "After that—we shall see."

"The senior footman—there are two or three of them, I believe—found him," remarked Harding. "His valet was away, on a holiday, and Green, the footman, was taking his duty. I'll get him in here."

He left the room, and presently returned with a young man who eyed the detective with a mixture of curiosity and apprehension. Charlesworth opened his book again.

"This is Green, eh?" he said. "What's your Christian name, Green? Edward? Well, you found Sir Charles dead this morning, didn't you? Just tell us about it—in your own way."

"Not much to tell about it, sir," replied Green. "Sir Charles' valet is away, so I was doing his work. I took Sir Charles his tea at the usual hour this morning—seven o'clock. I set down the tray on a table at his bedside, and went to draw the blinds up, and to do one or two other little things. Sir Charles didn't speak to me—as he had done other mornings—so I went up to the bed, thinking to wake him; he was particular about being up at seven o'clock. Then I saw there was something wrong, and I touched his hand. It was cold as ice, sir—and so was his forehead: I touched that, too. So I ran and called Mr. Bedford, the butler. That's all I know, sir."

"Thank you," said Charlesworth. "Ask Mr. Bedford to come here."

Bedford, the solemn-faced person who had received the detective, was a dapper and precise-looking man of apparently about thirty-eight or forty years of age. At Charlesworth's bidding he took a seat by the desk, evidently well aware of what was expected of him, and quite prepared to talk. And to begin with he corroborated what the footman had just said.

"Green fetched me from my room at a minute or two past seven," he replied in answer to Charlesworth's opening question. "I hurried to Sir Charles's room at once. I saw he was dead as soon as I reached the bedside. He was lying in quite a peaceful attitude, gentlemen, but there was a look about him—you understand? And he was as cold as ice."

"What did you do?" inquired Charlesworth.

"I telephoned immediately—there is a telephone in Sir Charles' bedroom—first to Dr. Holmes, and then to Mr. Harding there," replied Bedford. "They were here in less than a quarter of an hour."

"Did you tell anybody in the house in the meantime?"

"No! Green and I kept the matter quiet. We got both gentlemen up to Sir Charles' room without anyone knowing. Afterwards, Dr. Holmes saw Mrs. John Stanmore, who is staying here, and he and Mrs. John broke the news to my lady."

"How did she take it?"

"I can't say as to that, sir: I don't know. I have not seen her ladyship at all this morning. Dr. Holmes gave strict orders that she is not to be disturbed."

"Well, now, about last night. Did you see Sir Charles last night?"

"I didn't—I never saw him at all. The last time I saw him alive was yesterday morning, soon after nine o'clock, when he was setting off to town in his car, which he drove himself. He came home very late last night—later than usual. In fact, everybody had gone to bed. Sir Charles was very strict about rules and regulations. If he wasn't in by eleven o'clock no one, not even myself, was to sit up for him; he let himself in on such occasions with his latch-key. And last night he hadn't come in by eleven."

"Do you know what time he did come in?"

"I don't. I never heard anything of him. But my room is in another part of the house, and he always moved about very quietly when he came in late."

"You're quite sure there wouldn't be anyone up when he came in?"

"Absolutely positive, sir!"

"Do you know if anyone—any member of the family—saw him last night?"

"I'm quite sure that no one saw him—no one!"

"What about Lady Stanmore? Wouldn't she see him?"

"No! Sir Charles had his own suite of apartments; Lady Stanmore has hers. His was on the west side of the house; hers on the south. And Lady Stanmore had gone to her rooms long before eleven last night, and Mrs. John Stanmore had retired, too. I'm quite certain that nobody saw Sir Charles after he came in—no one," repeated Bedford, with emphasis. Then, after a moment's pause and hesitation, he added: "But I think I ought to tell you gentlemen something that's in my mind—I am strongly under the impression that Sir Charles did not come in alone!"

"Ah!" said Charlesworth. "You think he brought somebody in with him?"

"I do—I feel sure of it!"

"Why, how?"

"Because when I came into this room—his study, as you see—this morning, I found on this very desk two drinking glasses that had most certainly been used. There were other things too—a decanter of whisky, a syphon of mineral water, a box of cigars, a box of cigarettes. I am quite sure from these facts that Sir Charles brought somebody in with him."

"Would there be anything unusual in that?"

"Well, it wouldn't have been an extraordinary thing, but it would have been a thing of very rare occurrence. I am convinced, however, that he wasn't alone when he returned home. The mere presence of those two glasses, both of which had been used——"

Charlesworth suddenly interrupted the butler with sharp glance and a sharp question.

"Of course," he said, with a certain anxiety, "you've taken care of those glasses, haven't you?"

CHAPTER II
THE DECANTER

The butler was quick to notice the tone of concern in Charlesworth's voice, and his own, in reply, took on a note of dismay.

"I'm afraid not, sir!" he answered. "It never struck me—of course, there was nothing to arouse any suspicion in my mind, at that time: I just thought that Sir Charles had happened to bring a friend in for a drink. I fear the glasses will have been washed up, in the ordinary course. You wanted them?"

"Finger-prints, perhaps," said Charlesworth. "However——"

"There was something I noticed about those glasses, though," interrupted Bedford. "One of them had had whisky in it—in fact, there was a small amount of whisky and soda left in the glass. But the other glass had had no whisky in it."

"Did Sir Charles drink whisky?" asked Charlesworth.

"Yes, sir. He always had a glass or two every night before he retired."

"Then the glass which had had whisky in it was probably his?" said Charlesworth. "And that which hadn't, the other man's? What about the decanter, Bedford?"

"I have that, sir—just as I found it this morning."

"Let me have it—fetch it now, and it shall be sealed up," directed Charlesworth. He turned to Harding as the butler left the room. "We'll have that analysed," he said. "The poison may have been introduced into the whisky. And if so, it looks as though somebody in this house had had a hand in it. By-the-bye, as I suppose you know all about this family, what's it consist of? Nobody in the house but Sir Charles, his wife, and his sister?"

"Sister-in-law, Mrs. John Stanmore," replied Harding. "Of course there are servants. And there's a secretary—Miss Fawdale."

"If he's been poisoned, the thing to find out is—motive," remarked Charlesworth. "Now," he went on as Bedford came back with a small cut-glass decanter, in which about a quarter of a pint of whisky still remained, "you take charge of that, Superintendent, and have it sealed up and labelled, to hand over for analysis.

Well—what's next? This, I think. You're absolutely certain, Bedford, that is, as certain as you can be, that nobody in this house ever saw Sir Charles after he came in last night?"

"I'm positive of it!" declared Bedford. "I made the fullest inquiries this morning, after we found him dead. Nobody saw him—nobody heard anything of him."

"But—his car? Who attended to that?"

"He'd see to it himself, sir. He always did, when he came home late. There's a chauffeur, of course, but Sir Charles very rarely made use of him—he attended chiefly to my lady. There are three cars in the garage—Sir Charles, for his own purposes, used one which he's had some years and always drove himself. It was one of his rules that if he wasn't home by ten o'clock, Watson, the chauffeur, was not to wait up for him—he'd put his car in the garage himself. He did that last night. Watson went to bed at ten-thirty last night—Sir Charles hadn't come then."

"It just comes to this, apparently," remarked Charlesworth, turning to Harding. "Sir Charles came home late last night and nobody saw him. But there's some evidence that he brought some person into the house with him and that they had a drink in this room. Well now, Bedford, can you tell me this? Were the decanter and the mineral water and the glasses left here, in readiness for Sir Charles, or would he have to fetch them, himself, from another room?"

"I can explain that at once, sir," replied Bedford. "In addition to our footman, we have a parlour-maid, Purser. It was her duty, every night, when Sir Charles didn't come home to dinner—which, as a rule, was about four nights a week—to leave here, in his study, a tray, on which was a plate of sandwiches, another of biscuits, a decanter of whisky—which she fetched from my pantry—a syphon of soda-water, and a couple of glasses."

"Why a couple of glasses?" asked Charlesworth.

"Because every drink that Sir Charles had, he'd have a clean glass for it," replied the butler. "He wouldn't drink, sir, two glasses of sherry out of the same glass. As a rule, I believe, he never drank more than one glass of whisky before going to bed, but if he had a second, he'd have a clean glass for it."

"I see! Well—did Purser bring the tray in as usual last night?"

"She did—exactly as usual. We always knew, of course, when Sir Charles wasn't coming home to dinner. He was a great man for his club, Sir Charles—dined there three or four nights a week."

Charlesworth turned to Harding.

"I think we'd better see the parlour-maid," he said. "Perhaps Mr.

Bedford will send her in?"

Bedford rose, giving the two officials a somewhat peculiar and significant look.

"I think I'd better bring her in," he said. "She's a rather superior young woman, Miss Purser—she might feel a bit strange if——"

"Oh, bring her yourself, by all means," exclaimed Charlesworth. "There's no need for any secrecy: I only want to ask her a question or two which she'll no doubt easily answer. You can stop here when you bring her, too."

Bedford went off, to return in a few minutes with a pretty, smart-looking young woman, of apparently five and twenty years of age, who glanced at the two men waiting to receive her with a look that was half inquisitive and half demure. Charlesworth inspected her carefully as she took the seat which Harding drew forward, and decided that Bedford had been quite right when he described her as being something rather superior: he made a mental note that the parlour-maid was self-possessed, wary, cool, and probably keenly observant of everything that went on around her.

"I just want to ask you one or two questions, Miss Purser," he said. "I understand that it was one of your duties to leave in this room when Sir Charles happened to be dining out and not home till late, a tray of light refreshments for him. Yes?—well, did you leave it last night?"

"I did, sir!"

"What was on the tray?"

"The usual things. Sandwiches, biscuits, whisky, soda-water."

"Where did you get the whisky?"

"Where I always get it—from Mr. Bedford."

"Was the decanter full?"

"Three parts full."

"Were there two glasses on the tray?"

"Two tumblers—yes."

"Where did you get those?"

"From the butler's pantry. The tray is always ready for me there, at half-past ten, on evenings when Sir Charles is out—I mean was out."

"So you'd nothing to do but bring it in here?"

"That is so."

"Where did you put it last night?"

"Where I always put it—on this small table at the side of the desk."

"What time was that?"

"Twenty-five minutes to eleven."

"There was no one in this room, of course, when you brought in the tray?" said Charlesworth. "Empty, eh?"

Purser, for the first time, hesitated. She looked from one man to the other.

"Come!" continued Charlesworth, encouragingly. "Don't keep anything back!"

But Purser still hesitated, this time looking at the butler. Bedford nodded.

"I should do what Mr. Charlesworth asks," said Bedford. "Of course, I don't know what it is—you've said nothing to me."

"Listen!" said Charlesworth. "You no doubt know that there'll have to be a coroner's inquest in this affair? You'll be called as a witness, and you'll be on oath, and you'll have to tell everything. So—you may as well tell me . . . if there is something to tell. I asked you——"

Purser suddenly spoke.

"There was somebody in the room!" she said.

"Who?" demanded Charlesworth.

"Lady Stanmore! She was reading, in that chair."

"When you brought the tray in?"

"When I brought the tray in."

"Did she speak to you?"

"No. Not at all."

"You set the tray down and left her there?"

"I set down the tray and left her there."

"Did you close the door when you went out?"

"Of course!"

"What did you do, then?"

"Went to my room."

"Did you see anything more of Lady Stanmore?"

"How could I? The servants' quarters are in quite another part of the house."

Charlesworth glanced at his notes and turned to Bedford.

"You told us—here's what I wrote down—that Lady Stanmore had gone to her rooms long before eleven last night," he said. "How does that fit?"

"She'd gone before ten minutes to eleven, anyway," declared Bedford. "I saw Mrs. John Stanmore come out of the drawing-room at a quarter to eleven and go up the big stairs in the hall, and I saw my lady a minute or two afterwards come along the corridor and follow her. That's what I mean by long before eleven—a good ten minutes before."

"What time did you yourself retire?" asked Charlesworth.

"Just after eleven—a few minutes after."

"I suppose Sir Charles would let himself in with his latch-key? But you've no idea what time he came in, eh?"

"Not the least idea," replied Bedford, with emphasis. "I'll make bold to say, gentlemen, that there's nobody in this house who ever heard anything of Sir Charles' coming home last night—nobody! But there's nothing unusual in that—he's come in hundreds of times without anybody knowing."

"Bit odd, that, though, isn't it?" asked Charlesworth. "What with family and servants there must be at least twelve or fifteen people in this house. It's queer that no one heard anything! What about the car?—did no one hear that arrive?"

"Nothing strange about that, sir," replied Bedford. "The garage is two hundred yards from the house, and there are thick shrubberies between. Sir Charles would follow his usual plan; he'd put up the car himself and then walk up to the house. And there was no need for him to enter by the front door. Look here, gentlemen." He moved across to a French window which opened from one corner of the room, and tapped the glass panels. "Sir Charles always carried a key to this," he said. "As often as not, he'd let himself in this way, from the gardens. My opinion, gentlemen, if you want it," continued Bedford, "is that Sir Charles came in through this window last night, and that he let the man he had with him out by this window. I've a reason for thinking so."

"What is it?" asked Charlesworth.

"Well, it's this," replied Bedford. "When Sir Charles let himself in, late at night, at the front door, it was his custom to slip a certain bolt after he'd entered. Now that bolt wasn't slipped this morning. So I conclude he came straight into this room, from the gardens."

"Very good reasoning," said Charlesworth. "Well, I think that's all I want from Miss Purser and you, Bedford, just now. A word, though—don't talk! You know what I mean?—there's this coroner's inquest to come off, and then—eh?" He turned to Harding when the parlour-maid and the butler had gone, and gave the superintendent a meaning look. "I don't like that!" he murmured in a low tone. "Don't like it at all!"

"Don't like—what?" asked Harding.

"The fact that Lady Stanmore was left alone in this room after Purser put the tray there," replied Charlesworth, pointing to the table. "That's bound to come out at the inquest, and it'll look ugly. It looks ugly now—if . . ."

"If—what?"

"If . . ." Charlesworth paused, glancing knowingly at his companion. "You live in the same village, Harding," he went on. "You must know and hear things. How did these people get on—Sir Charles and his wife? Ever hear, know, or notice anything?"

"Nothing, except that Sir Charles was—well, I suppose old enough to be her father," replied Harding, stolidly. "Still, he was a fine, handsome, well-preserved man."

"Never heard of any domestic differences, eh?"

"I? No! Never heard anything."

"Bedford," remarked Charlesworth, "told us that Sir Charles had his rooms in one part of the house; Lady Stanmore hers in another. Not usual, surely!"

"Can't say," replied Harding. "Not acquainted with the habits or peculiarities of these people. Seems a bit odd, certainly. Very pretty woman, Lady Stanmore."

"Never heard any scandal, eh?" asked Charlesworth. "No lovers—anything like that?"

"Not a word! Nothing's known in the village, anyhow."

"Well, I'll have to inquire into things a bit more thoroughly," declared Charlesworth. "I don't like what Purser told us. There was opportunity——"

He paused as a knock came at the door and a lady entered, with an inquiring glance at Harding. Harding sprang to his feet with a bow; Charlesworth rose, too. Harding turned to him.

"Mrs. John Stanmore," he said.

CHAPTER III
DOUBLE TESTIMONY

As he made his bow to her, Charlesworth took a good look at Mrs. John Stanmore; he felt it incumbent upon him to make himself well acquainted with the appearance of anyone who happened to be a resident of Aldersyke Manor at that particular time. He saw a little, compact, self-possessed woman, probably from forty to forty-five years of age, well-preserved, alert, sharp of eye—a woman, he decided, who looked business-like and even shrewd. Mrs. Stanmore inspected him, too, critically—through a pair of folding glasses which she detached from her gown and perched, leisurely, on the bridge of her high-arched nose.

"Oh!" she exclaimed. "The—er, officer you told me you were sending for from Scotland Yard, Mr. Harding? Mr.——"

"Detective-Sergeant Charlesworth, ma'am," said Harding.

"How do you do?" Mrs. Stanmore became gracious. "I hope you'll be able to help us in this dreadful business. Mr. Harding, I came in to see you because I've just been talking to Dr. Holmes. Of course, it has been between ourselves, but Dr. Holmes said I could mention the fact to you. Dr. Holmes is strongly of opinion that my brother-in-law has been poisoned!"

"Yes," agreed Harding. "He thinks so."

"Dreadful!" said Mrs. Stanmore. "Of course, this Dr. Salmon for whom he's sent, can say definitely if it is so or not. But—and this is really what I came in about—unfortunately, the rumour has got spread about the house! The servants——"

"Who's spread it, ma'am?" interrupted Harding, a little angrily. "I told Bedford——"

"Oh it's not amongst the upper servants!" said Mrs. Stanmore. "It's—well, from what I've heard just now, it's a general rumour. And—I may, of course, speak freely to you and to Mr. Charlesworth?—I'm afraid there's going to be sad trouble! Dreadful trouble!"

"Of what nature, ma'am?" inquired Harding.

Mrs. Stanmore, who had taken a chair near the window, with her back to the light, became silent, studying the pattern of the carpet.

"I suppose it will all have to come out!" she said at last, with a sudden sigh. "There'll be an inquest, of course, and questions asked, and all that sort of thing. The truth is, Mr. Harding, however unpleasant it may sound, that the servants know quite well that my brother-in-law and his wife didn't get on together. Incompatible!—that's the word. They had nothing in common—their marriage was a mistake, a failure—and servants find these things out. And—they talk."

"Talking now, I suppose?" suggested Charlesworth, quietly. "And—what about?"

Mrs. Stanmore gave her questioner a sharp look. Something in the detective's steady response impelled her to be candid.

"I'm afraid the servants don't like Lady Stanmore," she said. "They idolized Sir Charles—he was a very indulgent, generous master. They are throwing out—hints."

"How did they reach your ears, Mrs. Stanmore?" asked Charlesworth. "There would be a channel, of course."

"Well, through Mrs. Protheroe, the housekeeper. And," continued Mrs. Stanmore, throwing up her hand as if to fling off all further reserve, "if you gentlemen, as representing the police, want the plain truth—which, as I've already said, must come out—Mrs. Protheroe herself, and Miss Fawdale, Sir Charles' secretary—I've just left them together, after a terribly serious conversation with them—both assert that they know something which they absolutely insist, things being as they are, on telling to the police! What are we to do?"

"Let them tell!" replied Charlesworth. "Whatever it may be, if they are determined to tell it, they will tell it. And why not?—in the interests of justice. I suppose," he went on, with a smile, "they have already told you?"

"Well, yes," admitted Mrs. Stanmore. "They have! They insisted. And—it's very dreadful, and I don't know what to think. Such a scandal—such—I suppose you'll have to see them?"

"No doubt of it!" said Charlesworth. He looked at Harding. "Better hear what they've got to say now?" he suggested. "Trite saying!—but there's no time like the present."

Harding hesitated. Charlesworth sat watching him—a little contemptuous. He had already set Harding down as the sort of man who dislikes trouble, bother, worry—evidently all this was new to him; perhaps the first case of murder, or suspected murder, that he had ever had.

"Oh, well, if you think it necessary," said Harding at last. "Of course, if they've anything to tell, they could have told it at the inquest. But if you want to be beforehand——"

"I do!" interrupted Charlesworth. "What am I here for? Perhaps Mrs. Stanmore would be so good as to fetch these ladies? I say!" he continued, when Mrs. Stanmore had left the room. "There's something I want posting up in. Sir Charles Stanmore, now?—was he a knight or a baronet? I'm not up in those matters."

"Baronet," replied Harding, laconically. "Got his baronetcy some years ago—for public services."

"Then—who succeeds to the title?" asked Charlesworth. "You say he'd no son of his own. Is there any heir to the title?"

Harding nodded at the door through which Mrs. Stanmore had just vanished.

"Mrs. John Stanmore's son, Guy Stanmore," he replied. "Sir Charles' nephew. A mere lad—I should say he's—well, twenty, or twenty-one, at most."

"Is he here?" asked Charlesworth.

"No—he's in the Army. Subaltern. I forget what regiment," answered Harding. "I believe he's just now at Aldershot—was, anyway, last time I heard of him. Sir Guy now, of course. He's——"

The door opened again. Mrs. Stanmore came back, preceding the two women of whom she had spoken. And once more Charlesworth exercised his powers of observation, first upon the housekeeper, Mrs. Protheroe, and then upon the dead man's private secretary, Miss Fawdale. They were vastly different. Mrs. Protheroe, a rather more than middle-aged woman, of a very evident severe respectability, was a specimen of the prim and proper serving-woman in high place; she owned a rigid mouth and hard eyes; Charlesworth realized that a defaulting scullery-maid would have a stiff time at her hands. Miss Fawdale, however, was young—two-or-three and twenty, perhaps; pretty, demure, smartly dressed. And that she had been weeping that morning Charlesworth perceived at first glance. But Mrs. Protheroe's eyes were dry and hard, and her general demeanour denoted indignation.

Charlesworth turned to Harding with a whisper.

"Your job!" he murmured. "They know you!"

Harding looked at the housekeeper, doubtfully. It needed but a glance to see that this business was not to his taste.

"Mrs. Stanmore says that you and Miss Fawdale have something to tell, Mrs. Protheroe," he said. "If you think it's something really relevant——"

"I should say it's decidedly relevant, Mr. Harding," interrupted the housekeeper, with decision. "Considering what we in this house know of the relations between my late employer and his wife I think it's relevant beyond question!"

"I know nothing about their relations," remarked Harding.

"We do!" declared Mrs. Protheroe. "They'd been strained for some time. Sir Charles and Lady Stanmore didn't get on—they were the last people in the world to suit each other. There was no open—I don't know how to express it, exactly, but there were no what you'd call scenes. Still—it was known to us of the household. My private belief is that Lady Stanmore, for some reason or other, hated her husband! And now I'm going to speak straight out. I know for a fact—and so does Miss Fawdale—that of late Lady Stanmore has had a lover, and has been meeting him in secret!"

Harding said nothing. He looked as a man looks who, against his will, is asked to share in a disagreeable business. But Charlesworth spoke.

"You've evidence of that, Mrs. Protheroe?" he asked. "It isn't merely rumour?"

"I've evidence!" retorted Mrs. Protheroe. "So has Miss Fawdale. The best evidence anybody can have—the evidence of our own eyes. Seeing is believing!"

"Well?" said Charlesworth.

"Some little time ago," continued Mrs. Protheroe, "I happened to go for a walk one afternoon in Aldersyke Spinney. That is a wood which is Sir Charles' private property, and is entered from the grounds of the Manor. It's strictly preserved for game—no one is permitted to enter it, except from the house. A very romantic, picturesque bit of scenery—there are some ruins in it, of an old Priory or something of that sort. I was looking round these ruins when I caught sight of Lady Stanmore, in company with a gentleman. The fact is they were sitting on a fallen tree, near the ruins. I didn't know him—he had never come to the house in my time, and I've been here since before Sir Charles' marriage—since three years before, as a matter of fact. He looked to me like a professional gentleman—dressed that way, you know, not in the way gentlemen dress in the country. I should say he's about thirty years of age—a handsome, rather distinguished-looking man."

"Well?" repeated Charlesworth.

"I'm not going to deny that I put myself where I could see them, and they couldn't see me," continued Mrs. Protheroe. "I am Sir Charles' old servant, with a great deal of respect for him—he was very popular with all of us—and I considered it my duty. And my opinion was that those two were lovers. At any rate—though it was only once—I saw them kiss each other when they parted. So—there you are!"

"Well?" said Charlesworth. "There's more, of course."

"Yes!" assented Mrs. Protheroe. "A week later, I saw Lady Stanmore leave the house one afternoon and cross the grounds in the direction of the Spinney. I followed her. But—on this occasion I took Miss Fawdale with me: I happened to meet her just as I was going out. We——"

"A moment, Mrs. Protheroe," said Charlesworth. "Had you already told Miss Fawdale of what you'd seen on a previous occasion?"

"I had!"

"Well—go on, then. Miss Fawdale went with you."

"Yes—and we saw Lady Stanmore with this gentleman, at the same place. And that time there was no doubt about their being lovers."

"You have grounds for that statement, of course, Mrs. Protheroe?" asked Charlesworth.

"Of course!—or I shouldn't make it. They behaved like lovers."

"And Miss Fawdale also saw this?"

"Ask her!"

Miss Fawdale looked down demurely at her interlaced fingers.

"I saw—what Mrs. Protheroe refers to," she murmured.

"Couldn't help it," said Mrs. Protheroe. "It was there to see."

Charlesworth glanced at Harding. Harding was looking glum and worried. He shook his head.

"I don't see what all this has got to do with what we're inquiring into," he remarked, grumblingly. "Don't see it at all! Lady Stanmore's affair, all that—not ours."

"Perhaps Mrs. Protheroe considers it has a bearing?" suggested Charlesworth, turning to the housekeeper. "I think she does—eh, Mrs. Protheroe?"

"I do!" exclaimed Mrs. Protheroe. "For you haven't heard everything yet. Miss Fawdale has something to tell you of what she saw yesterday—only yesterday!—afternoon. As things have turned out—and it's being talked of already that he's been poisoned—I think you ought to know all about it."

"We're waiting to hear everything about it," said Charlesworth. "What is it, Miss Fawdale? Don't be afraid—and don't keep anything back."

Miss Fawdale braced herself for her task, letting it be seen that she had no taste for its accomplishment.

"I—I don't like having to tell this," she said, hesitatingly, "but

Mrs. Protheroe thinks I should. It is just this—I was in the Spinney again yesterday afternoon, and I saw Lady Stanmore then, in the same place—the same gentleman was with her. They—they behaved as when Mrs. Protheroe and I had seen them before. But what Mrs. Protheroe particularly urges me to tell you is that before they parted, I saw this gentleman give Lady Stanmore a small packet, done up in white paper——"

"Stop there!" interrupted Charlesworth. "How far away were you from these two?"

"Perhaps fifteen or twenty yards," replied Miss Fawdale, after reflecting.

"Where were you? Hidden?"

"I was in the ruins—looking out through a break in the masonry."

"Well? A small packet, done up in white paper. How big?"

"Oh, small—like the powder one gets from chemists."

"You could see that quite clearly?"

"Quite clearly."

"Well—anything else?"

"Nothing, except that he seemed to be giving Lady Stanmore some very particular instructions or something of the sort, about this packet."

"How long did you watch these two?"

"Not long. They were there when I went into the ruins. Just after he had given her the packet, they got up from the fallen tree on which they were sitting and went away into the thick part of the wood."

"And you didn't follow?"

"No—I returned to the house."

Charlesworth asked no further questions. The three women withdrew. And when they had gone Charlesworth turned to Harding.

"Superintendent!" he said. "We must see Lady Stanmore—and at once!"

CHAPTER IV
AT BAY

But Harding began to show obvious signs of dissatisfaction and annoyance. He had been restive during the whole time Mrs. Protheroe and Miss Fawdale were detailing their stories, and now he shook his head in palpable disapproval.

"I don't like this at all!" he said. "It seems to me that we're going too fast. What's it all amount to—this stuff we've just heard? Women's gossip!—tittle-tattle! And—another thing. We don't know yet that Sir Charles was poisoned. I think we ought to wait until we've heard what this Dr. Salmon has to say about it."

"No!" declared Charlesworth. "We must see Lady Stanmore. In justice to her she ought to know what's being said. And I want to know, from her, if there's something that I suspect."

"What's that?" asked Harding.

"Well—it's an idea that occurred to me," replied Charlesworth. "I want to know—I can find it out, without any direct question to her—if there's any jealousy or has been, between her and Miss Fawdale. See?"

"No, I don't!" answered Harding. "What do you mean?"

"Never mind! Now, come on—let us get hold of Mrs. John Stanmore again, and get her to see Lady Stanmore and tell her that you and I want to see her for a few minutes. Then," continued Charlesworth, "you can leave the rest to me."

Harding left the room, still protesting that he saw no use in this proposition, and Charlesworth, left alone, looked about him. It was evident, from what he saw, that Sir Charles Stanmore had used this room for business purposes. A big book-case, which filled one side of it, was given up entirely to law books and works of reference; the furnishings were those of a busy man's office rather than those of a leisured one's study. But Charlesworth looked most particularly at the desk, and finally at the big blotting pad which lay in its centre. The uppermost sheet of paper was white and clean, save for a line or two of writing which showed at the top left-hand corner—it looked as if somebody, having written a letter, had only impressed the lower half of the letter-paper upon the blotting pad. And Charlesworth, first ascertaining that each sheet was detachable, took the top sheet off and held it up against the light of the window. This enabled him to read the impression—evidently only part, the concluding part, of a sentence:

"therefore agree to give you an option upon it for seven days from this date at the price mutually agreed upon this evening,

(Signed) CHARLES STANMORE."

Charlesworth carefully folded the sheet of blotting paper in such a fashion that the impression should not be interfered with and put it in his pocket-book, and he had only just done this when Harding reappeared at the door and beckoned to him.

"She'll see us," he said. "Come this way. I shall leave the talking to you," he added, as Charlesworth followed him along the corridor and then up the main staircase. "I don't want to figure in it. From what little I know of Lady Stanmore, I don't think you'll get much out of her. And of course she'll be terribly upset—naturally. For my part, I don't think it seems decent to break in on a woman at a time like this!"

Charlesworth made no reply to that. He was curious to see Lady Stanmore. And as soon as he and Harding were ushered into her presence by Mrs. John Stanmore, he saw that the Superintendent need not waste any sympathy nor indulge in any sentiment: Lady Stanmore showed no signs of grief nor anything but complete self-possession, coupled with some slight annoyance.

"Well?" she said, a little testily, when the two men were fairly in the room. "What do you want with me, Mr. Harding? I can't tell you anything!"

Harding indicated his companion.

"Detective-Sergeant Charlesworth, my lady," he said. "He would like——"

Lady Stanmore turned on Charlesworth with a distinctly unfriendly glance.

"What do you want?" she demanded, with an unpleasant stress on the personal pronoun. "And who sent for you? I am mistress here, I believe——"

"Superintendent Harding sent for me," replied Charlesworth. "Probably because of what Dr. Holmes told him."

"Oh, I know!" retorted Lady Stanmore. "Holmes thinks that my husband was poisoned! Perhaps he was. Perhaps he poisoned himself. Perhaps some of his friends in London poisoned him. But what do I know about it? Nothing! And care less!"

Charlesworth remained silent, looking at the woman he had been curious to see. She had been writing, at a desk in a corner of her boudoir, when they entered, and she still sat there, pen in hand, half-turned towards her visitors, a half-defiant, half-contemptuous smile on her face. She was an undeniably pretty young woman, thought Charlesworth, perhaps a beauty in both face and figure, but there was something about her, a strange look of proud resentment, of secret anger, which struck him as dominating everything else. He set her down as a woman who for some time had been nursing and cherishing a grievance. And while he was wondering what to say to her, Lady Stanmore spoke again, sharply, addressing herself to him.

"What *do* you want?" she demanded. "I am busy!"

"To ask your ladyship a few necessary questions," replied Charlesworth. "I take it that you have nothing to tell me which would throw any light on the matter of Sir Charles Stanmore's sudden death?"

"Nothing!"

"When did your ladyship last seen him—alive?"

"Yesterday morning, from this window, as he drove off in his car."

"You did not see him last night?"

"Not at all!"

"There is some ground for believing that Sir Charles, when he came home last night, very late, brought some person into the house with him. Does your ladyship know anything of that?"

"Nothing whatever! How should I?"

"I have ascertained that you were in Sir Charles' study at a little after half-past ten last night. Is that so? Well, your ladyship did not remain there until Sir Charles came home?"

"Of course I didn't—I was here, in this room, before eleven. What are you really wanting to know? I tell you, I know nothing!"

Charlesworth hesitated a moment. Then he decided on candour.

"Since you ask me such a plain question, Lady Stanmore," he said quietly, "I'll tell you plainly what I want to know. I want to know the name and address of the man whom you have met on several occasions recently in the Spinney, on the other side of your grounds? Just that!"

He spoke this question quickly, but he was scarcely prepared for the effect it produced on Lady Stanmore before he had come to the end of it. Dashing her pen on the desk in front of her, she started to her feet, and crimson with anger, turned on her sister-in-law.

"Who has been spying on me?" she demanded furiously. "You've had something to do with this—you!"

But Mrs. Stanmore shook her head, calmly.

"Nothing of the sort, Eileen!" she answered coolly. "Utter nonsense!"

"Who, then?" exclaimed Lady Stanmore. She turned on Charlesworth. "Who told you that?" she cried, stamping a foot in her anger. "Who?"

"That, my lady, I shall not say," replied Charlesworth. "But I may as well tell you that I have evidence that on several occasions of late you have met a man in the Spinney, that you and he have been seen to behave as lovers do, and that only yesterday afternoon you were with him there, and that he was then seen to hand you a small white packet. I want to know who he is, where he lives, and what that packet contained. I think—in your own interests—you had better tell me."

He was watching her keenly all the time he spoke—and suddenly he saw that she was going to tell. Her whole manner changed with startling swiftness: she laughed, as if amused rather than frightened.

"Oh, well, Mr. Detective—I've forgotten your name already—I suppose I may as well tell you," she said, almost sweetly. "After all, I'm free now! The gentleman you ask about is my cousin, Jim Beck—Dr. James Beck, of Wimpole Street. And the packet contained some powders for sleeplessness. There!"

"Have you any of the powders left?" asked Charlesworth calmly.

"No! There were only two, and I took them both last night: one at eleven, and the other at two o'clock," replied Lady Stanmore. "Well—any more questions?"

Charlesworth rose from his chair.

"I am much obliged to your ladyship," he said. "At present—no!"

He was turning towards the door, and Harding was about to follow him when Lady Stanmore stopped them with a gesture.

"Stop!" she said, peremptorily. "Just wait a moment—and you, too, if you please, Marie," she added, turning to Mrs. Stanmore. "I want you all to witness something. Mr. Harding, please to ring that bell. And then—wait!"

Harding rang the bell; a minute or two elapsed; then the butler appeared. Lady Stanmore motioned him to enter.

"Bedford!" she said, quietly. "You knew a great deal about my late husband's affairs, didn't you?"

Bedford smiled enigmatically.

"Well—Sir Charles trusted me a good deal, my lady," he answered.

"Do you know what salary Sir Charles gave Miss Fawdale, Bedford?" asked Lady Stanmore. "I mean—*nominal* salary?"

"Yes, my lady. I witnessed the agreement—and read it. A weekly engagement, my lady—salary twenty pounds a week."

"Have you got twenty pounds in cash, Bedford? You usually have money for various purposes. You have? Very well, Bedford. Go down, see Miss Fawdale, pay her twenty pounds in lieu of a week's notice and tell her to leave this house within an hour. And Bedford—see that she goes! One hour from now! Do you understand, Bedford?"

"I understand, my lady! I'll give your ladyship's orders."

"And you'll see that they're carried out, too!" interrupted Lady Stanmore. "Stop!—don't go! I want to say something before you and Mrs. John Stanmore and these gentlemen of the police. That something is my reason for ordering you to turn Miss Fawdale out of this house. This—that woman was my late husband's mistress! She was his mistress before he married me—she has been his mistress ever since—she——"

"Eileen, Eileen!" exclaimed Mrs. Stanmore. "For Heaven's sake, think what you are saying, think——"

"I know what I am saying well enough, Marie," replied Lady Stanmore. "What I am saying is true. Bedford, you will carry out my orders! And there is a further order for you which you will be just as careful to carry out. You will give the housekeeper, Mrs. Protheroe, a month's wages in lieu of notice, and tell her to leave at once. You will do the same as regards the parlour-maid, Purser—you know at what terms she's engaged; I don't. But you will get rid of these three women immediately—do you understand, Bedford, immediately! Out of this house all three go before noon to-day! Now go, Bedford."

The butler went, and Lady Stanmore turned to the two men.

"I have a very good idea as to where you got your information about me," she said. "It was from one or other or all three of these women. Now you know what I have done with them. You also know what I have said, and what I *know*, about the relations of Sir Charles Stanmore and Miss Fawdale. I suppose there'll be all sorts of inquiries about Sir Charles' death?—an inquest, no doubt. Very well, I will give evidence at the inquest—and anywhere else, too, if it's necessary. And I will repeat, then, in public, what I have said to you in private, and then the world shall know what sort of man Sir Charles was! As for me, I thank God I'm free of such a man—free! Will you please go away?"

But Charlesworth tarried—to ask one practical question.

"You told me that your cousin, Dr. James Beck, lives in Wimpole Street, Lady Stanmore," he said, quietly. "Wimpole Street is a pretty long one!—do you mind giving me the exact number?"

"The number is 527A," replied Lady Stanmore, just as quietly. "You could have found it in the directory. My cousin is a well-known medical man."

Charlesworth went out of the room and found Mrs. John Stanmore and Harding whispering together. The lady turned and disappeared as Charlesworth drew near; Harding shook his head dismally.

"I knew no good would come of that!" he said, lugubriously. "It's going to lead to nothing but the washing of a lot of dirty linen in public!"

"If linen is dirty it's got to be washed," retorted Charlesworth. "And it matters little whether it's in public or private. Besides, don't you see, man, all that has just got to come out!—it's the sort of stuff that can't be kept secret. If what Lady Stanmore says is true about Sir Charles and his lady secretary, well, there's going to be a lot to investigate. But first thing, I'm off in my car to see this Dr. James Beck. I want to hear——"

There he was interrupted. A footman came along, with a message that Mr. Gilford, Sir Charles Stanmore's partner, had arrived from Lincoln's Inn Fields, and would like to see Superintendent Harding and Detective-Sergeant Charlesworth, at once.

CHAPTER V
WHERE IS IT?

Mr. Gilford was waiting for the police officials in his late partner's study—a little, elderly, obviously exceedingly upset and anxious man, who was almost breathless with excitement. He seized instantly on Harding.

"I came the moment I got your message," he said, plunging into rapid talk. "I didn't go to my office this morning—they telephoned down to me at home, so I got in my car and came straight here. Is it true that Sir Charles is dead?"

"Quite true, sir," replied Harding. "He was found dead in bed, early this morning."

"And,"—Mr. Gilford paused, looking an inquiry which he seemed afraid to put into words—"and—your presence, and this gentleman's, seems to indicate that there's some suspicion of—not foul play, surely?"

"Dr. Holmes thinks that Sir Charles was poisoned, sir," said Harding, "and that the poison wasn't self-administered, either. He's sent for Dr. Salmon, to consult on the matter."

Mr. Gilford looked his horror. His anxiety deepened, palpably.

"Just tell me all you know, briefly," he said. "I suppose you've been inquiring into things already? Is—is anyone suspected?"

Harding nodded at Charlesworth, and the detective gave Mr. Gilford a concise account of everything that had taken place since his, Charlesworth's, own arrival that morning.

"As regards Lady Stanmore," he concluded, "I am not going to say anything at present, Mr. Gilford—I propose to call on her cousin, Dr. Beck, during the day. What I should like to get at is some clue as to the identity of the person who undoubtedly came home with Sir Charles Stanmore last night. For I feel convinced that somebody did come home with him. Can you throw any light on that? Do you know of anyone with whom he had an appointment?"

"No!" declared Gilford. "I do not! But——" he paused, looking at Harding. "Has any examination been made of the clothes which Sir Charles was wearing last night?" he asked. "If he was home late, he would be wearing the suit he wore yesterday in town. Has that been examined?"

"Yes, sir," replied Harding. "I ran through the pockets to see if I could find any clue or memorandum as to where he'd been yesterday evening. I didn't find anything. There was just what you'd expect to find—the usual things that a well-to-do gentleman carries. But no papers that yielded any information. Everything I found is locked up in a drawer in Sir Charles' bedroom. I have his bunch of keys, too. I've made no use of them, so far."

Mr. Gilford remained silent for a moment, evidently deep in thought.

"You didn't find anything in his clothes and in the room that struck you as being particularly valuable?" he asked, anxiously. "Jewellery, for instance?"

"Nothing beyond his own gold watch and chain and a very fine diamond ring," replied Harding.

Mr. Gilford again kept silence for a while. Then he turned to the two men and threw out his hands.

"Well, gentlemen!" he said. "I may as well tell you that Sir Charles, to the best of my belief, ought to have had on him, or there ought to be somewhere in this house, an article of extreme value! To put it in plain words, a certain diamond necklace, worth—I don't really know what it's worth, but at least twenty-five or thirty thousand pounds! I'd better tell you all about it, for the mere fact of his possession of it may have had something to do with his death. A few days ago—three days, to be exact—our client Lady Verringham, the Countess of Verringham, you know, called to see Sir Charles. I was in his room when she was shown in, and as she knows me very well, she asked me to remain while she told Sir Charles her business. She produced a magnificent diamond necklace which she said was her own private property—not an heirloom of the family—inherited from her mother. She said that she wished to sell it, to the best advantage, and knowing that Sir Charles had influence and business connections amongst diamond merchants she'd brought it to him, to do the best he could with it. He accepted the task!—very much against my wishes: I wanted him to send Lady Verringham to somebody who would be professionally interested; it didn't seem to me the proper thing for a solicitor to peddle precious stones. But Sir Charles was a man who always had his own way. He told Lady Verringham she'd brought the goods to the right place, gave her a receipt for the necklace, and put it—it was in a small morocco leather case—in his pocket. And, gentlemen, when he left the office yesterday afternoon, at five o'clock, it was still in his pocket! I know it was, for he took it out, just before leaving, showed it again to me—his reason was to draw my attention to the beautiful old setting of the diamonds—and put it back. And the question is now—where is it?"

Charlesworth had listened to all this with deep interest; Mr. Gilford's story aroused new ideas, new possibilities in his mind. He made no reply to the solicitor's question, but Harding made the obvious one.

"I should think he'd lock it up when he got home, sir," he said. "There's a safe there, in that corner, and I suppose there'll be a key in this bunch. I'd better hand these keys over to you?"

"Well, as I'm his partner, and am also one of his executors," replied Gilford, "I suppose you had. What is imperative is that we should at once make an exhaustive and thorough search for that necklace. Now tell me—is there anyone in the house, any member of the family, any servant, who saw Sir Charles after he got home last night?"

"No, sir!" said Harding. "There's no one. Sir Charles was not seen by anybody in this house last night after his return."

"That is—as far as we know," remarked Charlesworth. "We have not been able to ascertain that anyone did see him. But," he turned to Harding and smiled, "we don't know for a positive fact that somebody didn't!"

"My information," retorted Harding, a little resentfully, "is that nobody did! I've no evidence that anybody did."

"Well, I must examine the contents of that safe," said Gilford. "And in fact every place in which he might have deposited the necklace. And I must see Lady Stanmore and Mrs. John Stanmore—probably he showed the necklace to both. It's got to be found!"

The two police officials stood by while Gilford opened the safe and examined its contents. The diamond necklace was not amongst them. Nor was it in any of the drawers in the dead man's desk, nor in a cabinet that stood close by, nor anywhere in that room. Nor was it in any drawer or cupboard in his bedroom, nor in his dressing-room. And neither Lady Stanmore nor Mrs. John Stanmore, duly interviewed and questioned by Gilford, had seen or even heard of it.

Gilford turned despairingly to Charlesworth.

"You say you feel convinced that Sir Charles brought some person in with him last night?" he said. "Is there any proof of that beyond the two used glasses? Because, you see, he might have used both glasses himself."

"Yes—I thought of that, too," replied Charlesworth. "But I have some other proof. Here it is!" and he brought out the sheet of blotting paper, and explained how he had found it. "It looks to me," he went on, "as if Sir Charles had brought some man here in the hope of doing a deal with him about that necklace, and as if he had agreed to give the man an option on it. But—in that case, would he allow the man to carry it away?"

Gilford, frowning over the piece of blotting paper, shook his head.

"I don't know—I don't know!" he answered, fretfully. "Sir Charles was very, very careless in some things—extremely careless! Most unbusiness-like, in fact—from my point of view. He was the sort of man who would have and would go his own way. Well—how to find the man?"

"If he's an honest man, he'll come forward at once, on hearing of Sir Charles' death," said Charlesworth. "But I am going to town now, and I want to make some inquiries about several matters. Just give me a little information, if you please, Mr. Gilford. You say Sir Charles left your office in Lincoln's Inn Fields yesterday afternoon at five o'clock, with the necklace in his possession? You're sure of that?"

"Positive—absolutely positive! He had the morocco case in his hip-pocket."

"Where would he go?" asked Charlesworth. "We know he didn't come home to dinner."

"I know where he would go, and what he would do, if he followed his usual habits," replied Gilford. "I say if, mind you! He would walk to his club in Pall Mall—the Royal Automobile. He would probably have a swim there—he might afterwards amuse himself with a game of squash rackets or of billiards. He would dine there and perhaps spend the rest of the evening there. Eventually he would go to the garage where he always kept his car, get it, and drive himself home."

"Where is that garage?" asked Charlesworth, getting out his note-book.

"Fisher's, in Stillman's Mews, Haymarket," replied Gilford. "He always put up his car there—had done so for years."

"I'll make some inquiries at the club and at the garage," said Charlesworth. "Just a word, Mr. Gilford. You heard what we told you as regards the charge that Lady Stanmore brought against Sir Charles and Miss Fawdale? Can you say anything about that?"

But Gilford's face became impassive. He shook his head, determinedly.

"Nothing, sir!" he answered firmly. "I know nothing of my late partner's private life—nothing! Nor do I want to—unless I am compelled!"

Charlesworth went out to the powerful car in which he had come down from London. Harding came up to him in the hall.

"You'll be passing the police-station," he said. "You can give me a lift as far as that—it's at the further end of the village. This is a strange case!" he went on as the car moved off down the drive. "I don't know what to make of it! Do you?"

"Not yet!" replied Charlesworth. "But we're only beginning. There's one thing that rather puzzles me that you could perhaps clear up, Superintendent. If Sir Charles brought some man home with him last night, it was in all probability from London. Now, how did that man get away from the Manor? Sir Charles didn't drive him back, I fancy. Yet, he must have gone back since he wasn't in the house this morning."

"He could get away from this village easy enough," replied Harding. "There are two stations here—on different lines. And there are late trains from both. He could get trains at half-hour intervals up to 12.30 midnight, and there's another on one of the lines at 1.15."

"Make inquiries at both stations, will you?" said Charlesworth. "I shall be back from town during the afternoon, and we'll go more thoroughly into things. And no doubt by that time the doctors will have something definite to say, and then we shall be able—hullo, who's this?"

The big car slowed up suddenly, at the lodge gates, where a smaller car, driven by its single occupant, a young man, had just come to a halt, the driver bending over the side to speak to a lady whom Harding and Charlesworth suddenly recognized as Miss Fawdale.

"It's Sir Guy—the new baronet!" whispered Harding. "I suppose his mother telephoned for him. Good morning, Sir Guy!" he continued, obsequiously, as the young man glanced across at him and nodded. "Sorry you've had such bad news, sir—unexpected. . . ."

The new baronet stared, frowningly, from Harding to Charlesworth.

"Mr. Gilford got here yet?" he asked surlily.

"He has, Sir Guy!" replied Harding. "You'll find him in the study, Sir Guy. And if there's anything that you want me for, sir, if you'll 'phone down to the police-station——"

Sir Guy Stanmore made no answer: he was plainly in anything but a good temper. He moved his car forward, leaving a clear passage through the lodge gates for Charlesworth's, and turned again to Miss

Fawdale.

"Nice sort of young man!" remarked Charlesworth. "Good manners, eh?"

Harding heaved a deep sigh.

"I wish I'd his luck!" he said. "He's come into a nice thing, I'll bet!"

"Yes?" asked Charlesworth. "In addition to the title?"

"I should say so," replied Harding. "There are no children. And Sir Charles always made a great fuss of this young chap—spoiled child, I should call him!—always had everything he wanted."

"Well, don't you spoil him any more!" said Charlesworth, with a sly laugh. "Don't soft-soap him too much."

"Got to—in these country parts," growled Harding. "You don't know—you town chaps. If you want to be comfortable in these places, keep in with the nobs! That's my motto, anyhow. Here's the police-station. Come in when you get back."

Charlesworth nodded his assent, and went on towards London; an hour later he stood in the waiting-room of Dr. James Beck's house in Wimpole Street. Dr. Beck, after the fashion of medical men, visited in their own domains, kept him waiting longer than Charlesworth liked or approved of. But at last he came, Charlesworth's professional card in his hand, and looked wonderingly from it to Charlesworth. And Charlesworth saw at one glance that Dr. James Beck neither knew what he had come about, nor that Lady Stanmore's husband was dead.

CHAPTER VI

FROM NINE TILL ELEVEN

While Dr. Beck gazed inquiringly at him, Charlesworth looked narrowly at Dr. Beck. He prided himself on being a pretty good judge of character and what he saw in Beck's face made him resolve on a policy of candour. Beck, he felt sure, was the sort of man to whom you could speak straight out.

"You're wondering what I'm here for, doctor?" he began. "Not as a patient, sir!—I'm here on the sort of business indicated by my card. I'll go straight to the point, if you please. You are, I believe, related to Lady Stanmore, of Aldersyke Manor?"

Dr. Beck showed his surprise.

"Yes," he replied. "I am Lady Stanmore's cousin."

"Have you had any news from Aldersyke Manor this morning?" asked Charlesworth.

"News? No! What——"

"Sir Charles Stanmore is dead, Dr. Beck. He was found dead in bed early this morning."

Charlesworth watched Dr. Beck with renewed keenness as he made this announcement. But he saw no more surprise or astonishment than one would expect to see from anybody under such circumstances.

"Dear me!" exclaimed Dr. Beck. "That is very sudden! As far as I am aware—and I saw Lady Stanmore only yesterday—Sir Charles was in his usual good health——" He broke off at that, glancing again at Charlesworth's card: "You are, I see, from the Criminal Investigation Department," he continued. "Is there some suspicious circumstance——"

"I'll be perfectly plain with you, doctor," said Charlesworth. "As I've just said, Sir Charles was found dead in bed this morning. Dr. Holmes, of Aldersyke, was called at once. He formed the opinion that Sir Charles had been poisoned—and that the poison was not self-administered. So the local police notified our people and I was sent down immediately. I've just come from the Manor—on purpose to see you."

"Why me?" asked Dr. Beck.

"I'll continue to be perfectly plain," replied Charlesworth. "After my arrival, the local superintendent of police, Harding, and I made certain inquiries. We had some information placed before us which concerns you. I am going to tell you exactly what that information is: I am also—for I've no doubt it will all be made public at the necessary inquest—going to tell you the names of our informants. Mrs. Protheroe, the housekeeper at Aldersyke Manor, and Miss Fawdale, Sir Charles' secretary, told us that you have been in the habit of meeting your cousin, Lady Stanmore, in the wood known as the Spinney, and that you and she on these occasions have behaved as lovers. Further, Miss Fawdale says that she saw you and Lady Stanmore in the Spinney only yesterday afternoon, and that she saw you give Lady Stanmore a white packet. That," concluded Charlesworth, "is the whole of the information given to us concerning yourself. I'm acting on my own responsibility in giving it to you, and if you like to say anything——"

"As regards Lady Stanmore and myself," interrupted Dr. Beck, "I shall say nothing—that is my private business, and hers. As regards the white packet, that is easily explained. When I saw Lady Stanmore a few days ago, she complained to me of suffering from sleeplessness. Yesterday, before going to see her, I got my dispenser to make up two powders, which I took with me, and gave to my cousin. That is all there is to tell about that. But now tell me, if you please—has all this, this information as you call it, of Mrs. Protheroe's and Miss Fawdale's been communicated to Lady Stanmore?"

"It has—we told her precisely what I have just told you, doctor."

"What did she say about it?"

"At first, she was furiously angry, but almost immediately her attitude changed, and she became—I suppose contemptuous. At any rate, she very speedily took her revenge on the housekeeper and the secretary and also a parlour-maid, Purser!"

"May I ask how?"

"She summoned the butler and ordered him to turn all three out of the house! There and then!"

Dr. Beck became silent. But he continued to look steadily at his visitor.

"Oh!" he said at last. "Well—since we are being so very candid—did Lady Stanmore give any reason for that drastic proceeding?"

"She did in the case of Miss Fawdale," replied Charlesworth. "As regards the other two, I think Lady Stanmore felt that they'd been spying on her."

"But—Miss Fawdale?"

"That was certainly different! In the presence of Mrs. John Stanmore, Bedford, the butler, Harding, and myself, Lady Stanmore said that Miss Fawdale was Sir Charles Stanmore's mistress—had been his mistress before his marriage, and had remained his mistress ever since. Just that!"

"Well," remarked Dr. Beck, quietly, "from what I have heard from my cousin, I believe that allegation to be a perfectly true and possible one—I don't think there's any doubt about it. Sir Charles Stanmore was an unprincipled man of bad moral character, and he treated his young wife abominably! She is well rid of him!"

This was the first remark which Dr. Beck had made that had anything of warmth in it, and Charlesworth shook his head.

"I only hope it mayn't be said, or hinted at, that she got rid of him, doctor!" he murmured. "This is a queer case, and——"

"Between ourselves," interrupted Beck, "she was going to get rid of him in quite a different fashion—through the courts. She was only waiting for a certain amount of evidence."

"Miss Fawdale?" suggested Charlesworth.

"I had rather not say more," replied Beck. "She is free now! But—you?"

"What I am after at present is to find the person, whoever it was, man or woman, who accompanied Sir Charles Stanmore home last night," answered Charlesworth. "Of course, the whole thing is only beginning."

"Lady Stanmore is at the Manor?" asked Beck. "Very well, I shall take my sister, who lives with me here, and go down there at once. And if there is anything I can do to help you——"

"Nothing just now, thank you, doctor," replied Charlesworth. He left the house and walked round the corner towards the nearest cab-rank, muttering to himself. "He's all right!" he said. "That was the truth about the powders, no doubt. But—what about her ladyship? If Sir Charles was all that Beck says she may have thought a short cut preferable to a long one—and anyhow, she was in that study, alone, when Purser took in the tray last night . . . and Purser left her there!"

Although he had said nothing to Harding about it, Charlesworth, from a very early stage of his inquiries, had experienced a species of perhaps sub-conscious suspicion of Lady Stanmore. He felt sure that Holmes—though Holmes had been careful not to say so, explicitly—was absolutely certain that Sir Charles Stanmore had been poisoned: therefore, somebody had poisoned him. And evidently, from all he had heard and learnt, Lady Stanmore had wished to be free of her husband. Again, Lady Stanmore had certainly had an opportunity, the previous evening, of putting poison in the whisky which she knew her husband would drink on his return home. Charlesworth had known of more than one serious case that had been built up out of far more flimsy materials than these; he saw how he himself could very easily formulate a charge against Lady Stanmore.

But there was the unknown visitor of the previous midnight, and the mystery attaching to his visit—if it was a man. Sir Charles Stanmore's own movements must be traced first, and to begin the tracing Charlesworth drove down to the Royal Automobile Club in Pall Mall. Knowing that this was one of the most popular clubs in town and that its membership was a heavy one, he anticipated some difficulty in tracing Sir Charles' doings on the preceding evening. But when he had got hold of an accommodating official he found his task comparatively easy. Sir Charles, as usual, had arrived at the club about 5.30 the previous afternoon. He had been seen in the bar, in the billiard-room, in the smoking-room, in the reading-room at one time or another between that hour and 8.0 o'clock, when he entered the dining-room and sat down to dine at his usual table. All this gave Charlesworth no help: it was not until he had traced Sir Charles' movements up to 9.0 o'clock that he got some. Then he learned that just after 9.0 a gentleman called at the club and asked for Sir Charles Stanmore. Sir Charles just then happened to be crossing the big hall; the gentleman caught sight of and went after him; for a few minutes they stood talking, then they left the club together. Sir Charles did not return.

Charlesworth was now anxious to get an accurate description of the man who called. But though two or three attendants remembered the incident and the gentleman, not one could give a description likely to be of any use. He was a tall, well-built man. He was middle-aged. He was well-dressed. But whether he was dark or fair, had green eyes or bright yellow, coal-black or slate-grey, nobody knew. Only one attendant could say more than the general saying of the others, and he could but speak of a fleeting impression.

"Looked to me like a foreigner and a Jew, sir," he said. "That's how I put him down!"

However, the porter at the door remembered seeing Sir Charles Stanmore and his visitor leave; they walked away, he said, in the direction of the Haymarket. And as the garage spoken of by Gilford was that way, Charlesworth went off to it. He had no difficulty in getting information there. Sir Charles Stanmore, he quickly learnt, came to the garage at 11.0 o'clock the previous evening, got his car, and drove off in it. Was he alone? No—he'd a gentleman with him—a gentleman who came with him and went with him; in the car, of course. And when he had got some sort of description of him, Charlesworth had no doubt that this gentleman was the gentleman who had fetched Sir Charles Stanmore out of his club. But—where had these two, Sir Charles and his visitor, been between 9.0 o'clock and 11.0 o'clock; two hours? They had left the club together at, say, five minutes past nine and walked in the direction of the garage. But they could have walked to the garage in five minutes—yet they hadn't turned up there until eleven. Where had they been—and what doing—and had the doings of those two hours any bearing on Sir Charles' death some hours later? Charlesworth, however, had no clue to that, and after asking another question or two he got into his big car and told its driver to go back to Aldersyke Manor.

It was four o'clock in the afternoon when he once more reached the village, and remembering his promise to Harding, stopped his car at the police-station. A constable on duty within shook his head at sight of him.

"The Superintendent's up at the Manor, sir," he announced. "The Chief Constable came over this afternoon and while he was talking to Mr. Harding, Dr. Holmes rang up, asking the Superintendent to go up there and to take you with him, if you were here. So they both went up, and left word that if you came back you were to join them there."

Charlesworth went on to the Manor. There were three or four cars outside its front door. As his own drew up there, Bedford came out, looking as if he wished to speak. He drew Charlesworth aside.

"Mr. Gilford, Mr. Harding, the Chief Constable, and the two doctors are in the study, Mr. Charlesworth," he whispered. "I'm to take you there at once. Things have been happening since you left!" he continued, mysteriously. "I don't understand them! Sir Guy—as he is now—came just after you'd gone, but he didn't stop—I rather believe he'd a sort of scene with his mother, but I don't know what about. However, he went away again, very quickly—wouldn't have any lunch. And the three women have gone—Mrs. Protheroe, Miss Fawdale, Miss Purser. They left at once and two of them gave me pieces of their mind!"

"Which two?" asked Charlesworth.

"Protheroe and Purser! It was more in the way of hints—nasty hints," said Bedford. "Spite and malice, of course—but then, what they said to me, they'll say elsewhere—I know what women are, Mr.

Charlesworth, and what their tongues are, too!—don't I?"

"What did they hint at?" inquired Charlesworth.

Bedford looked round, as if to assure himself that they were alone.

"Well, it was really more than hints!" he said. "They're both saying—for that's what it comes to—that my lady poisoned Sir Charles! Pretty serious that, I think, Mr. Charlesworth!"

"The tongue is an unruly member, you know, Bedford," said the detective. "Ever heard that before? True, eh? Well, let me join these gentlemen."

Bedford took him along to the study. It required but one glance at the faces of the men whom he found there to realize that they were discussing a profoundly serious situation. Dr. Salmon, whom Charlesworth knew well enough, was the centre of the group, and he was evidently communicating the result of his consultation with Dr. Holmes: Charlesworth caught his last words.

". . . . . . that is my present conclusion," Dr. Salmon was saying. "I am firmly convinced that Sir Charles Stanmore died of poisoning, and that the poison was not self-administered. At present I cannot say what poison it was—that remains to be ascertained. But that he was poisoned—and probably, in plain language, murdered!—I am assured."

There was a dead silence. It was suddenly broken by Dr. Holmes.

"Gentlemen!" he said, in an agitated voice. "In view of what Dr. Salmon has just said, I feel bound, much against my will, to acquaint you with certain facts!"

CHAPTER VII
THE BORGIA CABINET

It was evident to every one of the five other men present that Dr. Holmes found it a very unpleasant thing to essay the task to which he felt himself compelled; he showed all the signs to be expected in a man who considers himself bound to discharge a disagreeable duty. That he wished what he was going to say to be kept secret was obvious from his covert glance at the door.

"It is with the greatest reluctance that I say what I feel absolutely obliged to say," he began in a low voice. "I have been wondering ever since Dr. Salmon came if I ought not to tell him at once—now, as Mr. Gilford is here, and Major Watkins"—he turned towards the Chief Constable—"I feel that I must tell. Mr. Gilford!—you, like myself, were present at Sir Charles Stanmore's wedding to the present Lady Stanmore?"

"I was!" agreed Gilford.

"You know who she was?" asked Holmes.

"Yes! She was a Miss Howison—Eileen Howison," replied Gilford. "Her father, if I mistake not, was of your profession."

"He was an Army doctor," said Holmes. "He belonged to the Medical Service of the Indian Army. When he retired, he settled down in London—it was at some reception to scientific persons in London that Sir Charles Stanmore met Miss Howison, who had gone to it with her father. I knew the father slightly—he came down here now and then after his daughter's marriage. I knew him as Colonel Howison. He is, of course, dead—he died three or four years ago. He was a very interesting man to meet, for he had lived a long time in India and being of a very observant nature and possessing a keen and well-trained memory, he had a great store of knowledge. But he was also something else!" continued Dr. Holmes. He turned and looked inquiringly at Dr. Salmon. "Does Colonel Howison's name not recall something to you?" he asked.

Dr. Salmon shook his head—but almost immediately shook it again, with an obviously different significance.

"I was going to say—no!" he answered. "But upon second thoughts, it does. Yet what, I can't at the moment say. Howison, now? What——"

"Colonel Howison was the greatest authority in his day on the poisons of the East!" said Holmes. "He was the author of a most learned monograph——"

"Ah, now I remember!" exclaimed Dr. Salmon. "Of course!—I have the book. Dear me!—and Lady Stanmore is Howison's daughter?"

"As we have said," replied Holmes, nodding towards Gilford. "Well, gentlemen, that is a fact! Colonel Howison knew more about the poisons of India and the East than I should think any man who has ever studied that subject, and, as I have just mentioned, he published a famous book on them. But what is more, and what is really pertinent at this juncture, is this—Colonel Howison possessed specimens of these poisons, at least of the more subtle ones. He kept them in a certain cabinet. And, at his death, that cabinet and his collection of books and papers dealing with this, his favourite study, passed into the hands of Lady Stanmore, his only child. And—they are in this house!"

Another dead silence followed on this announcement. The five men looked at Holmes with varying expressions. Then Major Watkins spoke.

"Do you mean to say, Holmes, that this cabinet has been preserved—here?"

"I do!" replied Holmes.

"With—with these deadly poisons left in it?"

"Yes! They were in it, anyway, when I last saw it."

"When was that?"

"Two or three years ago."

"Who showed it to you?"

"Sir Charles Stanmore. His wife was present. It was one night when I'd been dining here. We got talking about Colonel Howison. They showed me his books and papers and the cabinet. I remember a remark made by Sir Charles. 'There's enough stuff in that box, according to the old boy, to settle a regiment!' he said."

"Of course, they kept this cabinet securely locked—and locked up somewhere?" suggested Major Watkins.

"I cannot remember if Sir Charles Stanmore, or Lady Stanmore, unlocked it when it was shown to me," replied Holmes. "I know that I expressed considerable surprise that they should keep it at all!—but they only laughed at me. I know, too, where they kept it—I have never seen it since."

"Where did they keep it?" asked Major Watkins.

"In a very beautiful old Chippendale book-case which had belonged to Colonel Howison," replied Holmes. "It stood—and I suppose still stands—in the drawing-room, in a recess, and contains, in addition to the cabinet, Colonel Howison's collection of books on Eastern toxicology and kindred matters—a valuable collection."

Major Watkins turned to Gilford.

"Do you know anything of this, Mr. Gilford?" he asked. "Have you seen this cabinet?"

"I have seen the cabinet itself," replied Gilford. "And in the place and amongst the surroundings which Dr. Holmes describes, but I never knew what it contained; it was merely pointed out to me as a rare piece of Indian work. I believe I saw it—in the drawing-room—not so very long ago."

"Ring the bell, Harding," said Major Watkins. "We must see this thing at once, and it must be examined. Tell me," he continued, turning to the two medical men, "supposing the poisons in this cabinet had been originally deposited in it, say, twenty or thirty years ago, would they still be potent?"

But he got no opinion from either man; each shook his head mysteriously, and murmured that the poisons of the East . . . . .

"I see!" said Major Watkins. "Bit beyond Western knowledge, eh? We wish to examine something in the drawing-room," he continued, as Bedford appeared. "Please show us the way—and don't let us be interrupted when we're once there," he added. "Better guard the door yourself, I think."

Bedford ushered the six men into the big drawing-room, and closed the door on them; Holmes led the party up to a recess, in which stood a beautiful old book-case, filled with volumes in various conditions of excellence or repair. And in the centre of the middle shelf, with books close up to it on either side, stood a small square box, wonderfully carved, to which he lifted a pointing finger.

"That is it!" he said. "Just as I last saw it. I forgot to mention—Sir Charles Stanmore, when he brought it out for me to see, called it the Borgia Cabinet; the Borgias, he said, laughingly, would have delighted in it."

Major Watkins laid hold of the glass-fronted door of the book-case.

"Open!" he exclaimed. "Good God!—what folly! Kept where anybody, guests or servants, could get at it." He swung open the heavy door and stood aside. "I don't like handling even the outside of the thing!" he went on with a grimace. "Perhaps one of you gentlemen——"

Holmes stepped forward and taking the cabinet down from its shelf set it on a table close by.

"And this is open, too," he said quietly, lifting the lid. "And—there you are! There—are the poisons!"

The other men gathered round and gazed, fascinated, at the interior of the cabinet, from which, rising to their nostrils, came the faint, subtle scent of some Eastern wood. But they were chiefly interested in the arrangement of the interior. What confronted them was a device of twelve little cells, or compartments, in each of which was a small glass bottle, each bottle of a different tint or hue from the others. Each was fitted with a wooden stopper, instead of a cork, but none was labelled—the only distinction between each was the varying colours of the glass. The other five stood silently watching while Dr. Salmon carefully took out one bottle after another and held it up to the strong light of the window. He had examined five or six in this way when he suddenly came to one from which he at once withdrew the wooden stopper.

"This bottle has been interfered with, recently!" he exclaimed. "Certain of its contents have been poured out! Look! The lip of the bottle is still wet—sticky—it's a viscous fluid—and one side of the stopper is also damp where it has been put back against the wet and sticky place in the neck over which the fluid has trickled. I think we may conclude that—however, perhaps we had better not conclude anything at present. But—we must take away this cabinet!"

"And I, sir," said Charlesworth, turning to Major Watkins, "must ask to have this room locked up and the keys handed over to me. I want to make a thorough examination of it. There may be fingerprints on the doors of this book-case, and elsewhere."

"You and Harding can see to all that," replied the Chief Constable. He was still staring at the cabinet, over which the two medical men were bending and whispering together. "What criminal folly!" he exclaimed. "The idea of leaving a box full of that sort of stuff where anybody could get at it——Good Lord! there might have been children in the house who'd have meddled with it, some time or other. I suppose they really are poisons?" he concluded, suspiciously. "Not—just something else?"

"We will make sure of that—eventually," replied Dr. Salmon. "Now I propose to take this cabinet away with me, and by to-morrow, when I shall have to attend the inquest here, I shall perhaps have something more definite to say."

The Chief Constable led the way out; presently he and Harding went away; the two doctors retired into a room near the study for consultation, and Charlesworth was left alone with Mr. Gilford. And Gilford was upset, anxious, and querulous. It was plain to the detective that things were being too much for him.

"This is the most awful business I have ever had in my life, detective!" he exclaimed. "I scarcely know which way to turn or what to do next! My partner's death—and it may be murder!—is enough for one day, but no end of things seem to pile themselves upon it. That diamond necklace! This seeming suspicion about Lady Stanmore. Then Sir Guy—can't make that young man out. He came here this morning, in response to an urgent message from his mother, stayed about ten minutes when he got here, and went away again! Then these women being turned out of the house—that was high-handed conduct on Lady Stanmore's part, for they may be needed. However, they can be found—if necessary. But I seem to have a hundred-and-one things to do——"

"I'm afraid I shall have to trespass on your time, Mr. Gilford," said Charlesworth. "As you were Sir Charles' partner and are, I believe, his executor, or one of his executors, you're the only person who can give me some information I want——"

"Then you'll have to ask for it some other time, young man!" declared Gilford, "I must look through Stanmore's papers here, to-day. Come and see me in Lincoln's Inn Fields to-morrow morning. By-the-bye, you've been up to town. Have you heard anything whatever about the person who came home with Stanmore last night? Was there such a person, now?"

"I don't think there's the least doubt that Sir Charles brought a man home with him when he returned yesterday evening," replied Charlesworth. "But as to who that man was, I've learnt nothing!" He went on to tell of his doings at the club and at the garage. Gilford shook his head and groaned.

"Disappeared!" he said, dolefully. "He probably has the necklace! Well, he must be found, must! You had better get the Press to help you. Circulate a description of the man. He must be somewhere—somebody must know him. Besides, you're asking yourself a question—Where was Stanmore (and this man with him, I suppose) between 9.0 and 11.0 last night? Somebody must have seen them together. Oh, yes, get hold of the Press. And now let me get on with these papers."

Charlesworth went off to find Bedford: he wanted to know if Dr. Beck had arrived. Bedford, questioned on that point, looked his surprise.

"Dr. Beck, sir—Lady Stanmore's cousin? Yes, sir, he and his sister, Miss Beck, have been and have gone again!" he replied. "They took Lady Stanmore away with them—to their house in London. Wimpole Street is the address, Mr. Charlesworth."

Charlesworth concealed his surprise.

"Oh!" he said. "I see. Lady Stanmore's gone there, has she?"

"Leaving Mrs. John Stanmore—and myself—in charge, Mr. Charlesworth," replied Bedford. "Far better for her ladyship to be away from the house, sir, far better!"

Charlesworth nodded and turned away—to encounter the two doctors, who were crossing the hall. At sight of him they paused, exchanged a whispered word, and then motioned to him to accompany them to a side-door which admitted first to the gardens and then to a stable-yard. There, in a sunny corner, near a kennel, lay a dog, a big powerfully-built retriever, obviously of great age. At the sound of their feet it raised its head—and Charlesworth saw that it was blind.

"Charlesworth!" said Holmes. "You see this poor old chap?—he was a great favourite with Stanmore, who wouldn't have him destroyed, though he ought to have been relieved of his life months ago. Well—Stanmore's gone, and now—you understand?"

"You're not going to poison the dog?" exclaimed Charlesworth. "Poor old——"

"If what we surmise is correct," said Holmes, "he'll never know anything or feel anything!—and we shall learn a great deal. See here!—this scrap of meat is impregnated with the stuff out of that bottle—you know which—in the cabinet. Now watch—and I'm afraid, wait!"

The three men watched and waited after the old dog had swallowed the morsel of meat—watched him as he slept again in the sun. It seemed a long time. Suddenly he gave a deep sigh, stretched his limbs, lay still. Holmes pulled out his watch.

"Exactly fifty-seven minutes after swallowing it!" he muttered. "No spasm—no pain. Well—now we know!"

CHAPTER VIII
WHO STANDS TO GAIN?

The two doctors went away and Charlesworth returned to the house, wondering. Bedford met him in the hall.

"Would you care to join me in a cup of tea, Mr. Charlesworth?" he said. "Refreshing, sir—after all this worry. What's going to come of it, Mr. Charlesworth?" he continued as he led his guest into the butler's pantry and drew forward an easy chair. "Do the medical gentlemen really think Sir Charles was poisoned, now?"

"I don't think there's much doubt about that, Bedford!" replied Charlesworth. "I'm afraid it's certain! But as to who administered the poison—that's another question. There's a good deal of mystery in this case."

Bedford poured out the tea and handed a cup over.

"Been a good deal of mystery altogether about this house, sir, of late," he said. "Of course, it's not for me to speak, but between you and me, seeing that you're a police officer——"

"I wish you'd tell me anything you can," interrupted Charlesworth. "It's strictly between ourselves, of course. You were going to say——?"

"I was going to say, sir, that of late there's been something—well, something in the general atmosphere that's shown me there was unpleasantness afoot, all round," said Bedford. "It hasn't needed half an eye to see that relations were strained, very strained indeed, between the master and mistress. They haven't been what you'd call friendly for some time, and except when there's been a dinner party they've never had a meal together for weeks. Sir Charles, for some days before his death, had been in an uncommon bad temper—with everybody, though as a rule he was popular with the servants. Everything seemed to be going wrong—he was snappish and irascible. Only yesterday morning, before he went off to town in his car, I heard him having an awful row with Miss Fawdale in the study. The door was slightly open—I couldn't help hearing, though I didn't wait to catch anything particular—I was passing the study at the time. But when Sir Charles had gone I saw Miss Fawdale in tears—he'd an awful temper when roused, Mr. Charlesworth,

Sir Charles had!"

Charlesworth sipped his tea in silence for a while.

"Bedford!" he said at last. "You've been in Sir Charles' employ some time, eh?"

"Twelve years, sir."

"Before his marriage?"

"Oh, yes, sir—some years before that!"

"This wasn't a second marriage, was it?"

"Oh, no, sir—Sir Charles had been a bachelor until he married Miss Howison."

"Well, look here!—you heard what Lady Stanmore said about her husband and Miss Fawdale? That Miss Fawdale had been his mistress before he married Lady Stanmore and was so still? Do you think that's true?—was it so?—is it so?"

Bedford gave his guest an enigmatical smile and shrugged his shoulders.

"Can't say, Mr. Charlesworth, can't say at all, sir! How should I know? From what I've seen and heard, you'll say? Well, I wouldn't say—positively—from anything I've heard or seen. I know, sir—just what I do know!"

"And—how much does that amount to?" asked Charlesworth, smiling. "You've had opportunities, you know!"

"Not so many opportunities, sir, as you'd think," replied Bedford. "Sir Charles was one of those men, open enough on one side, but close as the devil on the other. I couldn't say anything, for certain. Of course, there were things that some people would have drawn conclusions from. But then, Mr. Charlesworth, as you know, some people make mountains out of molehills. And you remember what Shakespeare says—I read Shakespeare a good deal when I've time—

" 'Trifles light as air,
Are to the jealous confirmation strong
as proofs of Holy Writ.'

Wise man, Shakespeare, sir—if there ever was such a person!"

"What were the things that some people would have drawn conclusions from?" asked Charlesworth.

Bedford replenished his guest's cup and his own and passed over the buttered toast.

"Oh, well, sir, little things!" he said. "Miss Fawdale, sir, came here first about two years before Sir Charles was married. She was then, as near as I could guess, about eighteen years of age—very pretty girl. She came as Sir Charles' private secretary. From the first she had a suite of rooms here—the suite she had till this morning—and a maid to attend to her. As I said in Lady Stanmore's presence, and yours, I witnessed the agreement between her and Sir Charles. But that salary, sir, was—nominal! Miss Fawdale got a good deal more than that. In fact, you might say she'd everything she wanted. And—she did precious little work!"

"Was this going on when Sir Charles married Miss Howison?" asked Charlesworth.

"It was, sir. But after Sir Charles and Lady Stanmore came home from their honeymoon, there was a change. Miss Fawdale went to live in London—I believe she's a flat somewhere in the West End, but I don't know where. After that she was sometimes here, and sometimes in town. Of course, I could see that Lady Stanmore never liked her or her presence from the very first—but she had to put up with it; Sir Charles Stanmore, Mr. Charlesworth, was a man who never allowed any interference with his pleasure from anybody, not even his wife! Between you and me, sir, Lady Stanmore was a cypher in this house."

"You could gather something from Sir Charles' general behaviour towards Miss Fawdale," remarked Charlesworth. "How did he treat her?—in public?"

"He treated her, sir, as if she were one of the family—she might have been a younger sister, or something of that sort," replied Bedford. "To my mind, that would exactly explain his attitude. In fact, I've often wondered, sir, if she was some relation that Sir Charles was providing for. He made a great companion of her—she amused him, I think. Lady Stanmore didn't—cold, proud woman, Lady Stanmore, sir. But of course, she'd her reasons—and her troubles."

"Perhaps more than we know of," agreed Charlesworth. He remained silent a while, and then confronted the butler with a sudden question. "Bedford!" he said. "Do you know anything about that box, usually kept in an old-fashioned book-case in the drawing-room and called——"

"The Borgia Cabinet, sir?" broke in Bedford. "Lord!—there's none of us—the upper servants in this house, at any rate—that doesn't. Box full of the deadliest poisons, sir, collected in the East, chiefly in India, by Lady Stanmore's father, Colonel Howison, and left to her. We couldn't fail to know all about it, Mr. Charlesworth. There was never a house-party, or a dinner-party, here but Sir Charles used to pull out that cabinet, show it, and tell his guests that there was stuff in there sufficient to poison all London—it was a grim joke of his. Oh, yes—but Sir Charles always took care to keep the key of that cabinet himself, sir. I remember that when it and the books in the Chippendale case came, Lady Stanmore wanted to have the cabinet and its contents destroyed there and then—in fact, she'd given me strict orders to burn the lot myself. But Sir Charles stepped in and wouldn't hear of it. For some queer reason or other he was proud of that cabinet—might say, fond of it. Odd!—but he was. He was a bit eccentric, you know, Mr. Charlesworth."

"Well," observed Charlesworth, "the doctors have examined that cabinet, Bedford, and its contents, and from certain facts that came to light, they think that Sir Charles was poisoned by something taken from one of the bottles. Now who could have got at the cabinet? When we examined it just now, it was not locked, nor was the old book-case."

Bedford shook his head.

"Beyond me, sir! I'm wondering—wondering—do you know, sir, it's crossed my mind two or three times to-day—I wonder if, for some reason we know nothing of, Sir Charles took his own life? What do you think, Mr. Charlesworth?"

Charlesworth reflected. He had at first scouted the idea of suicide because there was no evidence of it in Sir Charles Stanmore's bedroom. But since witnessing the experiment on the old dog he had seen that the suicide theory was quite admissible. It had taken exactly fifty-seven minutes for the poison to work its fatal effect, and when the end had come it had been startlingly sudden, swift, painless. Charlesworth saw now how, if he wished to put an end to his life, Sir Charles, after parting with his visitor, could have gone to the drawing-room, got what he wanted from the cabinet, poured it into his whisky, drunk it off, replaced the little bottle in the cabinet, gone to bed and to sleep—and to die.

"Don't know what to think, Bedford," he said, rising. "But I've got to find out—somehow. Well, I must get back to town—see you to-morrow at the inquest."

"Long affair, I'm afraid that will be, sir," said Bedford. "Days and days, no doubt."

"Not to-morrow," replied Charlesworth. "Mere formal proceedings to-morrow. Just the opening and adjournment."

He went away late, and eventually back to headquarters. And after making a report there and holding a consultation with some of his superiors, he went out again—to seek the saloon of a certain tavern in a street off Whitehall, where, by means of a telephone message from Aldersyke Manor, sent earlier in the afternoon, he had fixed up a meeting with a man from Fleet Street. The man was there when he entered, and in five minutes he and Charlesworth, with glasses in front of them, were in a quiet corner.

". . . . and if it isn't a complete scoop for you, you, at any rate, have got the stuff first-hand from me," concluded Charlesworth after telling the reporter all that he at that moment wished to tell about the Aldersyke Manor affair. "There have been one or two of your kidney—local press, you know—hanging round during the day, and they may have got a few tips from the servants, and possibly from the local police, but you've got authoritative information. You'll make a big feature of it in to-morrow's issue?"

"Sure!" said the Fleet Street man. "Couple of columns, anyway—leave that to me!"

"Well, here's more I want you to do," continued Charlesworth. "This man who called for Stanmore at the club, who went with him to the garage, and drove away with him from there: I must get hold of him. Now listen!—he may have gone to the Continent. Can you get this stuff, some of it, anyhow, into the Paris papers, and say the Amsterdam papers, to-morrow morning? Can you, at any rate, get in a paragraph in those papers, begging this man, whoever he is, if he sees it, to come forward at once?"

"Nothing easier!" declared the Fleet Street man. "It shall be in every Parisian morning paper, and in every English paper in Paris, too, first thing to-morrow, and in the principal Continental papers as well. Again, leave that to me. And I say—keep me posted from day to day, or, better still, hour to hour. Press and police together, eh, Charlesworth? Admirable combination! Big case and great opportunity this for you, my boy! Good luck to you!"

Charlesworth agreed that the case was big and the opportunity great, and after dining in a Strand restaurant he went home to his modest bachelor flat in Bloomsbury to think things calmly over. But as he settled down over a pipe there came in to him one Robinshaw, a retired detective who, living close by, often dropped in of an evening for a talk. And to Robinshaw, as a man of experience, Charlesworth set forth, in detail, all his doings of the day.

"What do you make of it?" he asked, in conclusion. "What's your opinion?"

Robinshaw wagged his grey head.

"Ah!" he said. "Now you're asking me something! Well, there seems to be no doubt that this man was poisoned and by the stuff out of that cabinet. Now—is it suicide, or is it murder? It might be suicide. There may have been reasons for that—reasons that may come out yet. But if it's murder, you want to seek for the motive—the murderer's motive. From all you tell me, the wife had a motive—she was fed up with him and she has a lover. What more do you want?"

"But—the doctor, Beck, insisted that she was going to free herself by other means," pointed out Charlesworth. "That meant, of course, divorce."

"Maybe! But perhaps she got impatient. Perhaps she's one of these vindictive women who want revenge and aren't particular how they get it. There are such—plenty of 'em. And she'd the means at hand in that cabinet, and she knew, too, that it would be stiff work for anybody to prove her guilt. See?"

"Why?" demanded Charlesworth.

"Nothing but circumstantial evidence that I know of—from your account. Strong enough, no doubt, but no direct proof. From all you tell me, this Stanmore was notoriously careless about that cabinet——"

"Yes, but how the devil could some of that stuff get into his whisky unless it was put there on purpose!" exclaimed Charlesworth. "Come—come!"

"How do you know it was in his whisky? You don't—you're only supposing it was. What's more, in spite of what the doctors say, it mayn't have been that particular stuff, for all that the bottle was sticky and so on. You don't know anything except that he was poisoned. It's just supposition to say that the poison came out of that cabinet! Though—I daresay it did!"

"I'll bet it did—and out of that bottle, too!" muttered Charlesworth. "And it must have been somebody who knew all about the cabinet who made use of the stuff—I'll bet on that, too!"

"Well," said Robinshaw, "murders spring out of all sorts of things. This is the sort of murder—if it is murder—that's been planned. Now when murders are planned, the folks who plan them have some ulterior object. And so I'll give you a piece of sound advice, my lad! Find out if anybody, and if so, who, stands to gain by Stanmore's death!"

When Robinshaw had gone, Charlesworth, reflecting, realized how excellent was this counsel.

CHAPTER IX

WHAT'S IN THE WILL?

With the old detective's advice fresh in his mind, Charlesworth went round to Stanmore & Gilford's office in Lincoln's Inn Fields next morning and got an interview with Gilford. Gilford, as seemed to be usual with him, was irritable and grumpy: the sudden and mysterious death of his senior partner appeared to have thoroughly upset him.

"Well, what do you want?" he demanded when Charlesworth was shown in to him. "Found out anything?"

"Nothing of any great importance, Mr. Gilford," replied Charlesworth. "I've come to you for some information—information which, at this juncture, probably nobody but you can give and which we consider it's highly necessary to have."

"What information?" asked Gilford, testily. "I don't know of anything that I can tell you—I want to hear something from you!"

"We'll keep you posted, sir," said Charlesworth. "But there are things we can't get at—things you know all about, most likely. And what we want to know at present, believing it may throw a good deal of light on this affair, is this: who benefits by Sir Charles Stanmore's death?"

Gilford began shifting the papers about on his desk. He shook his head, with a variety of meanings.

"Why, as to that—do you mean financially?"

"Just what I do mean!" replied Charlesworth.

"Well, a good many people! Some of 'em substantially."

"He left a will, I suppose, Mr. Gilford?"

"He did!"

"Is it, may I ask, in your possession?"

"It is!"

"It would be a great help to us, Mr. Gilford, if you'd tell me exactly what its provisions are. May I know?"

"Is that what your superiors want? Are they asking about it at Headquarters?"

"It's been suggested to me that I should find out, from you, Mr. Gilford. You see, if there are people who, as you say, will benefit substantially by Sir Charles Stanmore's death, we'd like to know who these people are."

Gilford considered this proposition for a while in silence. Then he got up from his desk, produced a bunch of keys, and unlocked a safe.

"Well," he said, "of course, the will must be proved before long, and after that you or anybody else can get a copy of it at Somerset House. So I see no objection to giving you the information you want, Charlesworth. But for the present, it's to be kept secret, you understand?"

"Oh, certainly, Mr. Gilford," replied Charlesworth. "What we want is to know if we can get any clue from it."

Gilford swung open the heavy door of the safe and presently returned to his chair with a document tied about with red tape.

"This is the will!" he said. "It was made, in this office, about eighteen months ago. Now, again, all this, for the present, is between you and me, Charlesworth. To begin with, my late partner was a very rich man—the Exchequer will have a nice haul out of his death duties! He was not a millionaire, but he wasn't far off—worth, I should say, between eight and nine hundred thousand pounds: his father, the first baronet, was, of course, a very wealthy man. So you see, Stanmore had a lot to dispose of."

He began to turn over the sheets of the will, glancing here and there as he went along; Charlesworth waited in expectancy.

"I'm not going to inflict all the legal phraseology of this on you," said Gilford. "It will answer your purpose if I tell you the main contents, won't it? Well, before we get on to that, I may as well tell you that quite apart from anything bequeathed to her in this will, Lady Stanmore has a marriage settlement which secures to her £2,000 a year. You understand that?—a settlement made before their marriage. Well, in this will Sir Charles Stanmore leaves her £5,000 in cash, and £1,000 a year for life or until she marries again."

"Until she marries again?" repeated Charlesworth. "She'd lose it, in that event?"

"The £1,000 a year, yes. Not the bequest of £5,000 of course."

"What about the capital from which the £1,000 a year was derived?" inquired Charlesworth.

"That would go into the residue—with which I'll deal presently," replied Gilford.

"The settlement wouldn't be affected?" asked Charlesworth.

"Not at all! That stands against anything."

"She's all right, then, as regards money," suggested

Charlesworth. "But—I want to be clear about as many matters as possible—supposing that Lady Stanmore had run away with this cousin of hers, Dr. Beck—could the marriage settlement stand then?"

"Lady Stanmore hasn't and didn't run away with her cousin, Dr. Beck, my good sir!" replied Gilford, dryly. "So we can't suppose anything. As matters are, Lady Stanmore has her marriage settlement of £2,000 a year, a legacy of £5,000 and a £1,000 a year for life or until she marries. Also there is a gift of certain household furniture to her—but we won't bother about that."

"I think Sir Charles did pretty well by her!" murmured Charlesworth. "She's nothing to complain about, financially, anyhow!"

"No—quite nice provisions, I think," agreed Gilford. "Well, there's a legacy of £25,000 to Mrs. John Stanmore, Sir Charles' sister-in-law."

"Big amount!" commented Charlesworth.

"Yes—but Stanmore was very generous to his kinsfolk, and Mrs. John isn't at all well off," said Gilford. "I should say that he's probably provided for Mrs. John ever since her husband died, and of course he's borne all the expense of young Guy's education at Eton and Sandhurst—I know that for a fact. Made him a jolly handsome allowance, too, since he was gazetted. Well—as I say, £25,000 to Mrs. John Stanmore. And, next, a similar amount to Miss Fawdale—Miss Irene Fawdale."

"What?" exclaimed Charlesworth. "£25,000 to his—secretary? Isn't—isn't that an extraordinary thing!"

Gilford laid down the will, produced a snuff box, and took a pinch.

"Um!" he said. "On the face of it, it would seem so. But Stanmore was very fond of Miss Fawdale—in what way, I don't know."

"You know what Lady Stanmore said, before her sister-in-law, and before me, and before Bedford?" remarked Charlesworth. "Is it true? £25,000 is an awful lot of money to leave a secretary, unless——"

"My good sir!" interrupted Gilford. "Listen to me! I don't know if Lady Stanmore's charge against her late husband and Miss Irene Fawdale is true or is not true! What I do know is that I don't know it to be true. Also, I don't know it to be false. It may be true. It may be false. Probably nobody knows or ever has known whether it is true or is false except the two parties concerned. One of these parties is dead. He can't speak one way or the other. The one who's alive won't speak—you may be sure. Except, of course, to say that the whole thing is—moonshine!"

"But—that legacy?" said Charlesworth. "£25,000!"

"Oh, well, there it is—and the young woman will get it!" exclaimed Gilford. "Put it down to a whim of Stanmore's, if you like—though, of course, it was more than that—I tell you, he was fond of that girl in some way or other—I think she amused him—he found her good company. Now we go on to the next legacy—which is one of £1,000 to the butler, Bedford."

"Bedford, of course, had been with Sir Charles a long time," remarked Charlesworth. "Good old family servant!"

"Quite so—I think Bedford is deserving of his reward," said Gilford. "Well, then, £500 to the housekeeper, Mrs. Protheroe, and £500 to the parlour-maid, Elizabeth Purser. They'd been there some time, too. In addition to that, these two, and Bedford, will come in for still more under another provision. Sir Charles leaves £100 for every year of service to every servant, male or female, and every workman in his employ at Aldersyke Manor, and to every clerk in these offices who shall be still in employ at the time of his death. Very handsome!"

"Very handsome indeed!" agreed Charlesworth. "Not an ungenerous man, by any means, Mr. Gilford. And—-the rest, sir?

"The residue, you mean? Well," continued Gilford, "before we come to that there are some legacies, not of any great amount. £100 here, £50 there, to local charities and the like. There are also legacies of £1,000 each to the executors, of whom I am one. Now we come to the residue."

"Which, I suppose, amounts to a tidy lot, Mr. Gilford?" suggested Charlesworth, who had been making a mental calculation. "The great bulk of whatever Sir Charles had, I suppose?"

"It is as you put it, a tidy lot," agreed Gilford. "Well, the residue is left upon trust to Sir Charles' nephew, Guy Stanmore, for life, with remainder to his heirs entail male, whom failing, with remainders to various great charitable institutions—hospitals and the like. And—that's all."

"Sir Guy, then, is the principal beneficiary?" remarked Charlesworth.

"Exactly—as is only fitting, seeing that he succeeds to the title," replied Gilford. "Yes—the young man will be very well off. But now that you've got this information, has it given you any ideas?"

"A good many people are a great deal better off by reason of Sir Charles Stanmore's death," said Charlesworth with a smile. "Some of them considerably so! But there's another thing I'd like to know,

Mr. Gilford. I suppose nobody—nobody at all, except you, and perhaps the clerks in your office, has any idea of the provisions of that will, eh? Such things are always kept a dead secret, aren't they?"

A shade of annoyance crossed Gilford's face. He pointed to another document laid on his desk.

"They are, or ought to be!" he exclaimed. "But Stanmore was—I won't say a fool, for he was anything but that—well, he was careless, indifferent, about a lot of things—he'd no reserve where most men have no end of it. You see that document there? What d'ye think that is, young man? Nothing whatever but a word for word copy of this will! Where do you think I found it? On Stanmore's desk, yesterday! On his desk, I tell you!—not in a drawer, or in a safe, but on his desk, where anybody who entered his room (and he was never in that room during the day) could pick it up and read it! Never knew such carelessness in my life! I didn't know he had a copy. But I've found out this morning that he had a copy made when I was away on my holiday this year, and this, of course, is it. Lying on his desk!—just tossed there as if it had been of no importance—for anybody to pick up and to read! Did you ever hear of such—I don't know what to call it!"

"The question—to my mind—is, how long had it been there?" said Charlesworth. "It seems impossible that he, a lawyer——"

"Oh, but he was careless, careless!" exclaimed Gilford. "Exceedingly careless!"

"Perhaps he'd only taken it out of his safe—there is one, you know, in his study—that morning, and had forgotten to put it back?" suggested Charlesworth. "Of course, you don't know that it had been read——"

"Do you know that it hadn't?" interrupted Gilford. "Bless me!—several people would be in and out of that study during the day! And there are people who can't refrain from peeping and prying. Well, anyway, there's the fact!" He glanced at the clock. "Due at that inquest in an hour, you know," he remarked. "You going down? Then you'd better come with me in my car."

Harding was the first person they saw when they arrived at Aldersyke, and Harding took them aside.

"The Chief Constable and I have arranged matters with the coroner," he whispered, confidentially. "The proceedings this afternoon will be purely formal—identification—just a bit of evidence from Dr. Holmes and then an adjournment."

"For how long?" asked Gilford.

Harding glanced at Charlesworth, questioningly.

"We want to get evidence together," he said. "We thought of saying—a fortnight. Of course, if there are police proceedings before the resumed inquest——"

"Yes, just so," replied Charlesworth. "Ask for a fortnight's adjournment." He turned to Gilford as Harding went away. "For all we can do, and for all we can hear, we might just as well have stayed in town," he remarked. "The real interest will begin when the inquest's resumed—or if, as Harding says, we start anything in the police court. Nothing new to-day, anyway."

But half an hour later, as he and Gilford came out of the coroner's court, the inquest, at the coroner's suggestion, having been adjourned for three weeks, Charlesworth was suddenly aware of the approach of a big car which came at a rapid pace up the village street, pulled up, and discharged a tall, heavily-built, smartly-dressed man, who, after a word with a policeman came hurriedly towards Gilford.

"Mr. Gilford? Sir Charles Stanmore's partner?" he asked. "May I speak with you at once, Mr. Gilford? I have just arrived by aeroplane from Paris—arrived at Croydon, I mean, and hastened here by car. I learnt of Sir Charles' death this morning—saw it announced in the papers, you know—so I set off for England immediately by the quickest way—air! I am the man who came with Sir Charles to his house in this village the night before last, Mr. Gilford—my name is Mappleson, sir, Robert Mappleson!"

CHAPTER X
THE MIDNIGHT INTERVIEW

Gilford looked at the stranger as a man might look at another who has apparently dropped from the clouds. Then he indicated Charlesworth.

"Here's one who'll be very glad to hear whatever you have to tell, Mr. Mappleson," he said. "Detective-Sergeant Charlesworth, of the Criminal Investigation Department. He's in charge of this case—and has been very anxious to lay hands on you!"

Mappleson looked appraisingly at Charlesworth and smiled a little.

"Metaphorically, I hope?" he said. "Well, I hurried here as fast as possible—couldn't do otherwise after reading what I did in the papers this morning. Of course, I have a good deal to tell, gentlemen—perhaps what I can tell will throw some light on this affair. This inquest, now——?"

"Adjourned—for three weeks," said Gilford. "Come, let us all three go into Stanmore's study at the Manor; it's close by. I suppose," he went on, a few minutes later, when Bedford had admitted them to the house and received instructions that no one was to interrupt their conference, "that it was in this room you had your interview with Sir Charles Stanmore that night?—for you've already told us you came home with him. And before you tell us anything, Mr. Mappleson, I want to ask you a question which occurs to me just now. You were here!—that's settled. Do you think there's anybody at all, now that Stanmore is dead, who knows that you were here?"

Mappleson hesitated—hesitated so long that Charlesworth got inquisitive, and Gilford impatient.

"You don't seem certain—eh?" he said.

"That is a difficult question to answer, Mr. Gilford," said Mappleson, at last. "But I'll answer it. There are two people who know that somebody left this house some little time after midnight—that somebody being myself!—but they do not know who the somebody was! Nor do I know who these two people are! I can't give you any answer but that."

"We'd better hear your story," said Gilford.

"Exactly—before we come to what I've just told you of," assented Mappleson. "Well, my story is a very simple one. First, as to who I am. I am a diamond merchant, with one place of business in New York and another in Paris. I have been known to the late Sir Charles Stanmore for several years—fifteen years, I should say, and have done business with him on various occasions. One day last week, he, knowing that I was in town, wrote to me at my hotel, the Carlton, and asked me if I would call on him at his club—the date fixed was night before last. I did call—at just about nine o'clock, as near as I can recollcct. I caught him in the hall of the club. He took my arm and led me outside into Pall Mall. 'I've something of rare interest for you, Mappleson,' he said. 'Let's go across to your hotel and I'll tell you what it is—we shall be quieter there.' We went across to the Carlton, where I had a suite of rooms. I took him up and gave him a drink and a cigar. He then told me that a client of his, Lady Verringham, had placed in his hands, for outright disposal, a diamond necklace of historic interest, and he would like me to buy it. I replied that I would certainly like to see it, anyway. To my astonishment, he immediately produced the necklace from his hip-pocket!"

"Loose?" inquired Charlesworth.

"Oh, well, he had it in something or other," replied Mappleson. "Perhaps a case, perhaps a bit of soft leather—I forget. The point was that he was carrying it about with him—a valuable thing like that! For, with my thirty years experience and knowledge of diamonds, I saw at once that the necklace was of great value."

"What figure did you put on it?" inquired Charlesworth.

"Oh, well, really, that's rather a stiff question!" said Mappleson, smiling. "There was not only the intrinsic value of the necklace to be considered, but also the historic interest attaching to it, of which Stanmore had spoken. I don't know that I made any remark as to the value just then—at the Carlton, I mean."

"Still—what did you estimate the value of the diamonds at?" persisted Charlesworth. "You see, Mr. Mappleson, the necklace is missing!"

"Well," replied Mappleson, after a moment's consideration. "I should say at least thirty thousand pounds. I say—at least!"

"Yes?" said Charlesworth. "Continue, if you please."

"We discussed the necklace. I wanted to be sure that Lady Verringham really meant to sell—Stanmore assured me that she did and that he was empowered to conclude a deal without any further reference to her. Then he told me that he had at his house at Aldersyke—this house—a written memorandum of the history of the necklace, written by Lady Verringham herself. The necklace, he said, according to Lady Verringham's history of it, had had a very romantic career, and had at one time or another, belonged to various notable women, including one or two ill-fated royal personages. I expressed great interest in this, and said I should like to read Lady Verringham's memorandum—couldn't he send it to me? He immediately proposed that I should go with him, there and then, to see it—here. His car, he said, was in a garage, close by the hotel: he would race me out to Aldersyke Manor, I could look over the memorandum, and catch a train back to town. I demurred; it was growing late, and I was going across to Paris next morning by the 10.45 from Victoria. But you know what Stanmore was, Mr. Gilford?—the sort of man who insists on doing things there and then and persuades whoever it is he's dealing with to do what he wants. Anyway, he persuaded me, on this occasion, and we presently went round to some garage in the neighbourhood, got his car and set off to Aldersyke Manor."

"That would be—what time?" asked Charlesworth.

"At about eleven o'clock, as near as I remember," replied Mapleson. "It was nearing midnight when we got here. There was nobody about. The gates were open. Stanmore put his car in the garage—the lights of which were left on for him—himself; he remarked that he never allowed any of his servants to wait up for his return home, either outside or inside the house. We came through the grounds and the gardens to this room, and——"

"Pardon!" interrupted Charlesworth. "How did you enter? By the front door?"

"No—through that window, which was left open. As you see, you can step straight into or out of this room into the garden. The light was left on here, and on that small table there had been placed a tray on which were set out a decanter of whisky, a syphon of mineral water, two tumblers, and a plate or dish of sandwiches. On this desk lay a small pile of letters, and immediately on his entrance, Stanmore, excusing himself, turned them over. He singled out one. And now, gentlemen, I wish you to pay particular attention to what I am going to say. I don't think that Stanmore was a very good hand at concealing his feelings: he was apt, if anything vexed or annoyed him, to show them——"

"He was—quite right!" muttered Gilford. "Close enough about some things, but too open about others."

"Well, there was something in the letter he had singled out which evidently not only vexed but angered him, deeply," continued Mapleson. "His face became black as thunder—I saw him set his teeth with what looked like fury. But the storm passed as quickly as it had arisen—he crushed the letter back into its envelope and thrust that into a pocket. Then he turned to me, apologetically, and asked me to help myself to a drink and a mouthful of food. Now I don't drink, at any time; I took a half-tumblerful of the mineral water, and instead of a sandwich, a cigar which he offered. He mixed himself a stiff, I should say a very stiff drink from the decanter and the syphon, and wished me good luck. And I remember that when he had taken a deep pull at the stuff, he made a wry face and said there was rather a queer taste in the whisky—it must have gone a little stale in the decanter. But for all that, he drank it off, and then mixed himself a second tumblerful. And then he got out Lady Verringham's memorandum and handed it to me to read. I read it. While I read it, I kept an eye on him, too, for I saw he was upset about something—the letter, I supposed. He stood on that hearthrug, his hands thrust in his pockets, staring fixedly at his toes—he was evidently thinking deeply. Suddenly he came out of his reverie and turned to me, asking, abruptly, what I thought after reading the memorandum. We began to discuss the business side of the affair. Finally, I asked him to give me an option on the necklace for seven days. He agreed at once, and sitting down at that desk, he wrote out a formal agreement to that effect, which I have in my pocket. We talked a little more, and I had another look at this necklace—which, after this, my second inspection of it, he put back in his pocket. I remarked that I supposed he kept the necklace in that safe when he was at home. He laughed—not he, he said; it had lain on his dining-room table every night since he'd had charge of it. I expostulated, but he only laughed again. Then I rose to go—I had been at Aldersyke Manor before and I knew my way well enough through the village to the station. He let me out at this window—and closed it behind me as soon as I was outside: I distinctly remember hearing him fasten it. There was a strong light shining from it—the blinds and curtains were not drawn over it—to show me my way down the lawn to the main carriage drive. As I stepped on to that I turned and looked back. I could see Stanmore quite plainly through the window. He was standing by this desk, and he was again reading what I felt sure to be the letter that I have already spoken of. That was the last I saw of him."

Charlesworth was about to speak, but Mappleson held up a finger.

"Wait!" he said. "I have not finished. Now—considering all that has happened, and what I read in the papers this morning, and have read further in later papers as I motored from Croydon this afternoon—I have to tell of a further incident which may have some bearing on the mystery of Sir Charles Stanmore's death—it is for you, gentlemen, to decide as to that. As I turned the first corner of the drive—I was walking on the grass at the side of it, and I dare say making no sound—I suddenly saw, some yards in front of me, two figures. One was that of a man; the other that of a woman. I suppose that in the same instant in which I saw them, they heard me; anyway, in that same instant they vanished into the shelter of the trees on the edge of the drive—I heard them pushing a way into the undergrowth. I paid no attention; the thought that flashed across my mind was that this was some maid-servant keeping tryst with her lover, and I went on. But just outside the entrance-gates, perhaps twenty yards away, I saw, on the roadside, what seemed to be a big, powerful automobile drawn up, with some, at any rate, of its lights on. That, however, was not the way which I was going—my way lay in the opposite direction, and I had not much time to spare if I wished to catch the train. So I turned my back on this car, hurried to the station, got the train, and in due course returned to my hotel. And next morning I hurried over to France and to Paris. That is all, gentlemen."

"Much obliged to you, I'm sure," murmured Gilford. "A strange story!—strange, at any rate, in some parts of it. These two people in the drive, now—you couldn't see their faces, of course? No—a pity! And a big car, eh? That window? You say Stanmore fastened it when you left? Um! What do you make of it, Charlesworth?"

"Not easy to answer that question, Mr. Gilford," replied Charlesworth. "But I'm very glad to have heard Mr. Mappleson's story. It convinces me that the necklace was stolen in this house!—and of course, after Sir Charles Stanmore's death. That simplifies matters——"

"Not to me!" muttered Gilford. "Muddles them, rather! How does it simplify them?"

"We know all the people who were in the house that night," said Charlesworth, "and therefore——"

But the old lawyer interrupted him with a sly wink.

"Do we?" he said. "But perhaps we don't! Supposing the female figure that Mr. Mappleson here saw in the drive was that of a maid-servant, and the male figure that of some swell cracksman who was subsequently admitted by her to the house?—how does that strike you, my young friend? I think it very likely—but of course I'm not a detective!"

"I don't think it at all probable that a swell cracksman would have a big car on the roadside with its lights burning," replied

Charlesworth, smiling. "Afraid I can't agree there, Mr. Gilford. But I'm greatly obliged to Mr. Mappleson—he's established the fact that Sir Charles Stanmore had the necklace in his pocket when Mr. Mappleson left him that night, and presumably placed it once more on the table of his dining-room. One thing I would like to know—and probably never shall!—what and from whom was the letter that seemed to distress or upset Sir Charles? You weren't near enough to see the handwriting, Mr. Mappleson?"

"There was no handwriting," replied Mappleson. "I did see that. The letter was typewritten."

"And of course it has disappeared," said Charlesworth. "Sir Charles must have destroyed it, then and there. Nothing likely to upset him was found on his desk or in his pockets, I believe, Mr. Gilford?"

"Nothing!" answered Gilford. "I've examined all papers carefully, and——"

At this juncture Bedford tapped at the door and entering informed Gilford that Dr. Serracold, of Queen Anne Street, hearing that Mr. Gilford was in the house, would very much like to see him for a few minutes.

CHAPTER XI

MEDICINE—LAW

Gilford bade the butler show Dr. Serracold in; when Bedford had gone he turned to his companions with a shrug of his shoulders.

"Another development—or revelation—or suggestion!" he exclaimed. "More complications! It'll be a relief to me, Charlesworth, when you police people get this affair unravelled. What, now, can this Queen Anne Street man—some specialist, no doubt—have to tell us?"

"Every little helps, sir," said Charlesworth.

"Excellent platitude, no doubt, my friend!" retorted Gilford, sarcastically. "Well—it's for you to put all the little bits together. Come in, Dr. Serracold," he continued, as Bedford brought in a grave, elderly man. "I suppose you really came down to the inquest on Sir Charles Stanmore and finding it adjourned, came here?"

Dr. Serracold set down his tall hat, and taking the chair which Charlesworth drew forward, looked inquiringly at his questioner.

"Mr. Gilford, I presume?" he said. "The late Sir Charles Stanmore's partner? Yes, Mr. Gilford, you are quite right in your supposition. I came down to the inquest, which I had seen announced in this morning's newspapers, and, as you say, came to you on hearing that the inquest had been adjourned, and that you were at the Manor." He paused, glancing at Mappleson and Charlesworth. "I wished to have some conversation with you of a confidential nature, Mr. Gilford," he resumed. "These gentlemen——"

"You can speak before them, Dr. Serracold," answered Gilford. "One—that one—is the detective in charge of this case; the other is Mr. Mappleson, who is, as far as we know, the very last person who ever saw Stanmore alive."

Dr. Serracold regarded Mappleson with interest.

"May I ask when that was?" he inquired.

"About midnight—night before last," replied Mappleson.

"Was he—er, quite well, then?" asked Dr. Serracold.

"He appeared to be so, as far as I could see," said Mappleson.

Dr. Serracold rubbed his chin and turned to Gilford.

"The fact is," he said, "I felt it my duty, after reading what has appeared in the newspapers, to come down here and volunteer my evidence. As the inquest has been adjourned, I think I had better tell you, Mr. Gilford, what that evidence amounts to."

"If you please," said Gilford.

"You can make what use of it you like," continued Dr. Serracold. "The truth is—Sir Charles Stanmore, on his own initiative, having heard of me as a specialist in heart trouble, came last week to consult me about his heart, concerning which he had lately formed some suspicion. At his request, I examined him very carefully, and I also got him to answer my questions—searching questions—about himself. Also at his request, I told him the plain truth as to his condition."

"Forced you to do so, I suppose?" suggested Gilford. "He would!—I knew Stanmore and what he was like about things of that sort!"

"Well—he did! He insisted on my telling him the truth. So I told him."

"And what was the truth?"

"The truth was that his heart was in such a bad condition that while it was possible that with care he might live some time, it was also possible that under any great excitement, or undue strain, he might—and probably would—die at any moment," replied Dr. Serracold. "And that is what I wished to tell at the inquest. For I read in the newspapers that there is some suspicion of poison—I, from what I discovered during my examination of him, think it far more likely that Sir Charles died from heart failure, quite suddenly. Do you, does anyone know whether anything occurred on the night of his death, to upset him—irritate him—vex him—anything of that sort?"

Gilford glanced significantly at Mappleson, and Mappleson caught his meaning.

"He certainly was upset!" he murmured. "No doubt of it!"

"Ah!" exclaimed Dr. Serracold. "You observed—something?"

"I have just told Mr. Gilford that I returned here with Sir Charles that night," said Mappleson. "When we came into this room he found several letters on that desk, and he singled out and opened and read one of them. It was plain to see that its contents upset him—he gave every sign, though silently, of intense anger and irritation. But I am bound to say that it seemed to pass off as rapidly as it arose."

"Still, it was there," pointed out Dr. Serracold, triumphantly, as if Mappleson's reply had confirmed his theory, "and it would do him no good if, out of politeness to you, he suppressed it by a more or less strong effort of will. I feel sure that that is what really happened," he continued, turning to Gilford. "Heart failure! His heart was in a very,

very bad condition."

"There is evidence of poisoning," remarked Charlesworth.

Dr. Serracold turned to the detective, looked him over, and smiled.

"Of course, I am not in a position to know that," he said, superciliously. "I know nothing beyond the rumour. But I know what I know myself!"

"Perhaps, sir, you won't mind telling me this," said Charlesworth. "Supposing a man to have some serious affection of the heart, as you say Sir Charles Stanmore undoubtedly had, would that man be more susceptible to the effects of poison than a man whose heart was perfectly sound? I should be glad to know—if you'll be kind enough to tell me."

Dr. Serracold, still somewhat stiff and supercilious in manner, permitted himself one word in reply.

"Yes!"

"Thank you, sir," said Charlesworth. He glanced at Gilford. "I don't think there's any doubt, from what we know, that Sir Charles Stanmore was poisoned," he continued. "Still, Dr. Serracold's evidence as to the other matter will be useful—I'll see that you're called at the adjourned inquest, Dr. Serracold."

"Oh, yes—we must let the coroner know what Dr. Serracold has to say," agreed Gilford. "It helps. But I think I agree with Charlesworth—the evidence as regards the poisoning is too strong to be set aside. You see, Dr. Serracold, a good deal of what we know hasn't appeared in print, yet."

"Of course, I know nothing beyond what I have read," said Dr. Serracold, stiffly. "On what I do know, I think my theory a sound one."

He presently took his leave, and Gilford turned to his companions.

"We're finding out some queer things about Stanmore!" he remarked. "What next, I wonder?"

What Charlesworth heard next—and that was on the following morning—was from Gilford himself. Gilford telephoned to him at an early hour, asking him to go round to his office at once. And Charlesworth went, and found, closeted with Gilford, a man whom he knew at first sight, to be another limb of the law, and who was introduced as Mr. Pellick, of Bedford Row.

"You know what I said to you and Mappleson, yesterday, Charlesworth?" began Gilford. "That we were finding out some queer things about Stanmore? Well, here's something queerer than ever! Mr. Pellick, there, who's a well-known solicitor, and a friend of ours, has just told me a story with which you must be acquainted. You remember that I recently told you, in confidence, what the provisions of Sir Charles Stanmore's will were? Also that I have the will and am a trustee and executor under it? Well, it now appears that only the other day—last week in fact—Sir Charles went privately to Mr. Pellick, told him that he wanted to make a new will, wished him to prepare it, and after its execution, keep it secret, and gave him a memorandum, in pencil, of its provisions, so that Pellick might make a draft for his approval. And," concluded Gilford, spreading out his hands as a sign of his astonishment, "Pellick has shown me that memorandum and the new will—-had it been made—would have been strangely different to the old!"

"But—it wasn't made?" inquired Charlesworth.

"It wasn't made, of course! It got no further than I have just told you——"

"Stanmore was to have called to-day to see the draft," remarked Pellick, raising a folded paper which he held in one hand. "This is the draft."

"Do I understand that the old will stands?" asked Charlesworth.

"Certainly!" replied Gilford. "The new will can't even be said to have come into any existence. What is strange about it is that the dispositions of the will which Stanmore wished Pellick to prepare are—well, if not entirely different, at any rate vastly different to those of the old will. And I'm wondering if this difference will suggest any clue to the mystery of Stanmore's death?"

"Better tell Charlesworth how the wills vary," suggested Pellick.

"Give me your draft," said Gilford. He unfolded the big sheets of paper and turned them over. "Well, I'll explain," he continued. "Charlesworth, no doubt, remembers what the provisions of the old will—I call it that, but it is, of course, *the* will—are, and he can contrast them with these new ideas. To start with, there is no difference whatever between the two wills as regards the dispositions to Lady Stanmore—these are identical in both. There is none as regards the legacy to Mrs. John Stanmore. None as regards the legacies to Bedford, the servants, and the charities. But as regards Miss Irene Fawdale and Sir Guy Stanmore, the dispositions are not merely totally different, but amazing! Instead of Miss Fawdale getting a legacy of £25,000 she is given £500 a year for life! Instead of Sir Guy getting the residue—which I calculated at between eight and nine hundred thousand pounds—he is to have a like sum, £500, for life. A trust is created for these two annual payments, and at the deaths of the two recipients the capital sum is to be divided between any lawful children of each—that is, if Miss Fawdale marries, her children will get the capital represented by the £500 a year, and the same as regards Sir Guy. Now, what on earth, Charlesworth, had occurred that made Stanmore so change his mind? In the will that was made he gives this young woman £25,000 and his nephew an enormous fortune; in the one he wanted made he leaves them each a beggarly £500 a year! Extraordinary!"

"You haven't mentioned the residue—as he disposed of it, or wished to dispose of it, in the new will," remarked Pellick.

"Oh, the residue!" exclaimed Gilford, glancing at his sheets of paper. "I wasn't so much interested in that! However, this, Charlesworth, is what was to become of the residue if this new will had ever been made. One-third of the residue was to go to the Royal Society for the Prevention of Cruelty to Animals; one-third to the London Orphan School, and the remaining third to the Zoological Society. Whatever can one make of it?"

"But—it's of no effect, this draft?" inquired Charlesworth. "It doesn't set aside the old will—*the* will, as you term it?"

The two solicitors looked at each other. Each seemed to be waiting for the other to speak.

"Well," said Gilford, at last, "if this memorandum—this pencilled memorandum—of Stanmore's came into court, it might, I suppose, be argued that as it is in his handwriting, it certainly expressed his intentions at the time he drew it up. But it's not signed; it's not even initialled; it isn't even dated. I don't think it's of any effect?" he concluded, glancing at Pellick.

"No!" agreed Pellick. "In my opinion, none."

"What is interesting about it," said Gilford, "is this—as I said just now, what on earth had occurred to make Stanmore practically disinherit his nephew, and change his secretary's legacy from £25,000 to an annuity of £500 a year? Something! But—what?"

Charlesworth was thinking; thinking back.

"I heard something from the butler," he remarked. "He told me that on the morning before his death, he, Bedford, happened to overhear what he called a row between his master and Miss Fawdale. High words, and so on—Sir Charles, he said, was evidently in a temper. But he knew and could tell no more than that."

"And she probably won't tell," remarked Gilford. "Well, as to rows—I'm afraid there was nothing very new in that, as far as Stanmore's concerned—he was constantly in rows. He'd grown very touchy, irritable, and even bad-tempered; he used to row the clerks in the office here. But more amazing than the Fawdale business is the disinheriting—for it amounts to that—of young Guy! The lad succeeds to the baronetcy—nothing, of course, could alter that—and he was to keep it up on a miserable £500 a year! What had he done to offend his uncle?"

The two solicitors looked at each other and shook their heads. But Charlesworth after watching them for a minute or two in silence, laughed softly.

"But you say the old will is *the* will, gentlemen!" he said. "So—why trouble about the alterations which are of no effect? As things are, Miss Fawdale will get her £25,000, and Sir Guy Stanmore will come into the residue of close on a million! Am I right?"

"Oh, quite right, quite right!" said Gilford. "The will in my possession is *the* will!"

"The only thing that interests me," remarked Charlesworth, "is the questions you have been putting, Mr. Gilford. It's evident that during the last few days of his life Sir Charles Stanmore's feelings towards Miss Fawdale and Mr. Guy Stanmore had undergone some startling change. Why? He must have had some cause. What was it? And now—supposing I try to find that out?"

CHAPTER XII
THE LEATHER UNDER-JACKET

Full of a laudable intention to enter on this new voyage of discovery, Charlesworth went away from Gilford's office eager enough to carry it out. But he had not gone far before he realized that he was utterly puzzled. He was up against two questions which he couldn't answer. The first was—what was in that letter which, according to Mappleson, Sir Charles Stanmore found on his desk when he and Mappleson entered the study and which, in Mappleson's opinion, upset and agitated him considerably? And the second was—what had occurred within the few days immediately preceding his death which made him resolve on altering his will as regards his secretary and his nephew? A third question sprang out of these two. Were whatever was in the letter and the resolve to alter the will at all related?

After considering these problems over his mid-day dinner Charlesworth went off to Aldersyke and sought out Harding—to plump him with a straight question.

"Didn't Bedford call you up on the 'phone as soon as he found that his master was dead the other morning?" he asked.

"He did," assented Harding, "and I went there at once."

"Had anything been touched in Stanmore's room?" inquired Charlesworth.

"I should say not," replied Harding. "In fact, I'm sure. Bedford told me that as soon as the footman fetched him he immediately 'phoned me (there's a telephone in that room) and Dr. Holmes. We were both there, within ten minutes. And Bedford assured me that no one but the footman, Green, and himself had been in the room."

"Not even Lady Stanmore?" suggested Charlesworth.

"Lady Stanmore didn't know what had happened," said Harding. "She didn't know for some little time—a quarter of an hour, perhaps—after Holmes and I got there. Then Holmes went to break the news to her and to Mrs. John Stanmore."

"Did Lady Stanmore come to the room then?"

"No, she didn't! She never came near it. To the best of my belief," said Harding, with a significant glance at his visitor, "and as far as I know, Lady Stanmore never saw her husband's dead body!

She'd every opportunity, of course, but I believe I should be quite right if I affirmed positively that she never did see it."

"Well, look here," said Charlesworth. "Was the room in order when you went into it?"

"Quite! I should say Sir Charles was one of those very orderly men—systematic. Everything was very tidy—things in their place, you know. There was a dressing-room opening out of one side of the bedroom, and a bathroom opening out of another; everything was in order in both."

"You examined Sir Charles' clothing—I mean what he'd taken off the night before—didn't you? There and then, eh?"

"Well, it was certainly before I left his rooms. The suit he'd been wearing the night before was folded up on a stand in the dressing-room. I went through all the pockets, papers, everything, to see if I could get any clue. And as you know, Charlesworth, I didn't."

"Well—I'll tell you what it is, Harding! We've had information—never mind from whom, just now—that when he returned home that night Sir Charles found a certain letter awaiting him which, when he'd read it, or glanced over it, appeared to annoy and upset him. He was seen—seen, mind you, by our informant—to thrust it into a pocket. You found no letter of that sort? No letter that seemed to contain purely private news or information?"

"No—nothing whatever of that sort. Besides," said Harding, "you've already seen, yourself, everything that I found! I showed you the whole lot, soon after you got to the Manor that morning."

"He must have destroyed it!" muttered Charlesworth. He reflected a moment or two. "Oh well," he went on, presently. "I think I'd better tell you where I got the information I've just mentioned—it'll have to be given in public before long." He proceeded to repeat Mappleson's story from the diamond merchant's meeting with Sir Charles Stanmore at the club to his leaving Aldersyke Manor after midnight. "Now what do you think of that?" he asked in conclusion. "Who could the woman and the man be that Mappleson saw in the carriage drive?"

But Harding shrugged his shoulders.

"I don't think much about that," he said. "I should say that Mappleson's first impression was the correct one. A maid-servant meeting her sweetheart!"

"Is it likely—that time of night?"

"Why not? There are, or were, six or seven women-servants in that house. It was one of 'em. She could get out and in again, easy enough."

"But the car that Mappleson saw in the road was, according to his description, a big, powerful one—he saw enough of it to see that. Would the owner of such a car be meeting a maid-servant?"

"Come, come!" retorted Harding, with a laugh. "Where's your detective sense? It mightn't be the owner—it might be, and probably was, a chauffeur who'd taken his master's car out for a spree of his own! That's constantly done. I don't see anything in that part of Mappleson's story. But I do in the letter part of it—but I tell you I never found any such letter. And I believe Mr. Gilford has gone through all the papers he could find——"

"Oh, Gilford hasn't found it," said Charlesworth. "But I wish you had! It strikes me that there was something in that letter which might have given us a clue."

"Well, I didn't—and so there you are," declared Harding. He looked inquiringly at Charlesworth. "Do you think you're getting towards any solution?" he asked, half sceptically. Then, without waiting for an answer, he continued, shaking his head: "I don't believe it'll ever be found out!—I mean, I don't think you'll ever find out who poisoned Sir Charles—if anybody did!"

"What d'you mean?—if anybody did?" asked Charlesworth.

"Oh, I don't know! They're saying about here that he poisoned himself because he'd found out that his wife was carrying on with her cousin, Dr. Beck. Local talk!"

"Oh, that's out, is it?" asked Charlesworth.

"What do you expect?" replied Harding. "When Lady Stanmore bundled the housekeeper and the parlour-maid—not to speak of the secretary—out of the house that morning, she sent out two enemies who immediately proceeded to talk their tongues off! Good Lord!—don't you know anything about women?"

"Not much, thank goodness!" laughed Charlesworth. "Haven't had time. Great gossippers, I understand?"

Harding gave his visitor a look that was half-incredulous, half-pitying, and picking up a pen, turned to a letter which he had laid aside, half-written, when Charlesworth entered.

"Go away!" he said, smiling. "Go and learn something!"

Charlesworth laughed, and went. But instead of returning to town, he walked on to the Manor and asked for Bedford. The butler had little to do in these days, and was obviously glad to see him. He pressed hospitality on his visitor, but Charlesworth went straight to his point.

"I want you to let your memory go back:—it's not any great stretch!—to that morning of Sir Charles' death, Bedford," he said.

"You telephoned for Mr. Harding and Dr. Holmes as soon as Green had made his discovery, didn't you, and they came at once. Now, are you sure that nobody came into your master's room from the time you entered it until those two came?"

"No one came in, sir," declared Bedford. "No one at all! As a matter of fact, Mr. Charlesworth, nobody but Green and myself knew what had happened. I never left the room after entering it—there is a telephone there, you know. I remained in the room, and I kept Green outside the door. As soon as I saw Dr. Holmes and the police-superintendent coming up the drive I sent Green down to let them in and to bring them up. No—no one ever came into that room, sir—that's certain."

"Well, very soon after he and Dr. Holmes arrived, Harding examined your master's clothing, didn't he?" said Charlesworth. "I mean the suit he'd taken off the night before."

"He did, sir. In Sir Charles' dressing-room."

"Where is that suit now, Bedford?"

"In the dressing-room, sir. Nothing has been touched. The room's just as Sir Charles left it."

"Take me up there," said Charlesworth. "I want to have a look round."

Bedford took him upstairs and through the dead man's bedroom to the dressing-room. He pointed to a suit of dark grey tweed which lay, neatly folded, on a stand.

"That's the suit Sir Charles was wearing when he came home that evening," he said. "It is, of course, the suit in which he'd gone out the previous morning. I saw Mr. Harding go through all the pockets myself. The contents—papers, articles of value and so on—he took away: I think he sealed them up, downstairs."

Charlesworth looked speculatively at the tweed suit.

"Wouldn't Sir Charles be wearing an overcoat?"

"It was very seldom that Sir Charles ever did wear an overcoat, Mr. Charlesworth," replied Bedford.

"But surely," said Charlesworth, "motoring home at such a late hour . . ."

"What he did wear, supplementary like, when he was motoring, was this," Bedford continued, opening the door of a press, and pointing to a sleeveless jacket of leather. "He used to put that on under his coat, sir; he'd take it off when he got to the garage in town where he was in the habit of leaving the car, and put it on again at night when he came home."

"Would he have it on that night?" asked Charlesworth. "That particular night?"

"He had it on when he went off in the morning, Mr. Charlesworth," said Bedford. "That I do know. You see, as a rule, he never kept that leather jacket up here—he used to keep it in a little room in the hall where his boots were kept, and things like that, and just before going out, he'd take off his ordinary jacket and slip this on, over his waistcoat. He used to take it off when he came in, and hang it up in that little room. But on that particular night," continued Bedford, "he seems to have come up to his rooms in it. There it is, anyway."

"Do you know if Harding examined it?" asked Charlesworth.

"I don't remember seeing him do so," replied the butler. "I saw him examine the pockets of that suit. That lay where it is now—Sir Charles was very particular about folding up his clothes. Evidently he'd hung up the leather jacket in this press."

Charlesworth took down the leather jacket and ran his fingers over its surface. And instantly he recognized the feel of paper inside the left half of the front. Slipping his hand inside he found that there was a pocket there, and in the pocket a letter—he could feel the torn edges of the flap of the envelope. He glanced at his companion—Bedford's orderly mind had perceived something amiss in the arrangement of the room and he had turned his back to the detective. And in a second the letter had been transferred from the leather jacket to Charlesworth's pocket, and when Bedford turned again he was putting the jacket back in its place.

"Well," he said, indifferently, "if, in looking round, you ever find anything that seems likely to help, Bedford, let me know. Every little helps!—as I've said before."

"Rely on me, sir," replied Bedford. "Getting on at all, Mr. Charlesworth?"

"Oh, I daresay we shall worry through!" answered Charlesworth. "Stiff work—so little to go on, you know."

He left the Manor and walked down the village street till he came to the entrance to the churchyard. There was nobody about there, and he turned inside the old lych-gate and sitting on a bench in its shadow, took out his find and examined it. At the first sight of the envelope he let out a sharp exclamation—for the letter was addressed, not to Sir Charles but to Lady Stanmore.

On seeing this, Charlesworth immediately noted two or three things. First, the date, which was that of the day before Sir Charles' death; second, the postmark, which was London, S.W.; third, that the address was typewritten. And, as he expected, the enclosure was typewritten, too. He glanced round, to make sure that there was no one near who could steal up and look over his shoulder, and read the thing through from beginning to end.

"Lady Stanmore, Madam," it ran, "I think it my duty to inform you that for some time your husband Sir Charles Stanmore has been carrying on an intrigue with the young woman whom he passes off as his secretary, Miss Fawdale. I have made it my business to watch him and to follow his movements and I am in a position to report to you positively that whatever may happen when Miss F. is at Aldersyke Manor, what happens when she is in town is this. 1st, Sir Charles spends whole afternoons and evenings with her at her flat. 2nd, he constantly takes her for long motor rides in the country. 3rd, her establishment could not possibly be kept up on a private secretary's salary. If you desire me to give you further proof of these statements and to engage my services in procuring still more evidence, please insert an advertisement in the Personal Column of *The Times* worded XCB347 Eromnats, and I will communicate with you again."

Charlesworth folded up this precious epistle and put it carefully away in his pocket-book. In the course of his professional career he had seen letters of this sort before; he even had an idea that he knew the scoundrel who had written this in pursuance of a despicable calling. But he left that aside. What interested him was that he now felt certain that this letter had been placed on Sir Charles Stanmore's desk by Lady Stanmore herself—for him to see as soon as he came in that night!

CHAPTER XIII
I PUT IT THERE!

After reflecting on the possibilities arising through his discovery of this anonymous letter, Charlesworth returned to town, and going straight to Dr. Beck's house, asked boldly for Lady Stanmore. He was shown into a waiting-room, but when the door opened it was not Lady Stanmore who appeared but Dr. Beck. And Dr. Beck did not look over pleased or over friendly.

"May I ask your reason for wishing to see Lady Stanmore?" he inquired icily. "She is staying here with my sister and myself, to be sure, but she is not over well, and we wish to spare her——"

"You may be quite sure I shouldn't have called here to ask for Lady Stanmore if I hadn't had good reason, Dr. Beck," interrupted Charlesworth. "It is as much for Lady Stanmore's sake as my own that I did call! I am entrusted with this case and I am doing my best to clear it up, and——"

"There seem to be many matters in connection with it which need clearing up," remarked Beck. "As you are here, I should like to speak of one in which I seem to be concerned. When you were here before, you told me of what those women, Mrs. Protheroe and Miss Fawdale, had said—had told you, I think—about Lady Stanmore and myself? You remember?—that they had seen us behaving as lovers?"

"Yes," said Charlesworth. "Well?"

"Well, you know, that's all false! So far from being Lady Stanmore's lover, I am engaged to another lady, and am, as a matter of fact, to be married to her very shortly! So—there you are!"

"Then—those women were lying?" said Charlesworth.

"Call it what you please! All I say is that they were not stating the fact when they said that Lady Stanmore and I behaved as lovers. No doubt we exchanged a kiss on parting—Lady Stanmore and I are first cousins, and have always been on affectionate terms, for she never had any brother and looks on me as one, and in addition to that we were brought up together, as boy and girl. But those women had no ground whatever for their allegation."

"Why—if I may ask—did you meet Lady Stanmore secretly?" asked Charlesworth.

"If you like to call it secret! I don't know that it was meant to be secret. Sir Charles Stanmore was a man of such a violent nature—hasty, irascible, easily vexed and thrown into a passion——"

"He was, eh?" interrupted Charlesworth. "Ah, perhaps that explains—I beg your pardon, doctor. You were saying——"

"That his wife did not wish me to go to the house, especially as he and I had a hearty dislike for each other. My cousin wanted to see me about several things and—we met. That is all there is in that."

"Couldn't she have come here?" suggested Charlesworth.

"If you really want to know, Stanmore had forbidden her to come here. He had obsessions. One was that my sister and I prejudiced his wife against him. That wasn't true." Beck paused, looking Charlesworth carefully over. "I think I may speak freely and confidentially to you," he said, after a pause. "I think you're doing your best about this case, with nothing but a desire to get at the truth."

"Thank you, doctor," replied Charlesworth. "You've hit it!"

"Well, I'll tell you my honest belief—as a medical man," continued Beck. "And it is this—I believe, from all I have heard and have pieced together, that during the last two or three weeks of his life Stanmore was mentally deranged. If necessary I could give you proof of it—perhaps proof will have to be given. My cousin had a hell of a time with him—she puts it down to his bad temper, his irascibility, and so forth: I don't. I think he was—as I say, mentally deranged, in some form or other. And my honest belief as regards his death, is that he committed suicide!"

"You really think that?" exclaimed Charlesworth.

"I do! I think that you will find I am right, too."

"Well," said Charlesworth, after a pause, "I certainly don't seem to be finding out anything which lays the fault of murder at anybody's door! This is a very queer case indeed, doctor—several people might have put poison in Stanmore's whisky that night, but I can't find out any particular reason why any one of them should! Of course, if Lady Stanmore—you don't mind my speaking straight out?—if Lady Stanmore had been madly in love with you, and just as madly anxious to get rid of her husband, and as she knows all about the poisons in that cabinet which once belonged to her father—you follow me?"

"Oh, I follow you," said Beck. "But Lady Stanmore isn't and hasn't been in love with me, and as I told you before, she was going to obtain her freedom by another method, less dangerous and clumsy. Do you understand?"

"The divorce court, I suppose? That was really her intention?"

"Absolutely, it was! And at once."

"Over——" Charlesworth hesitated. "Over—Miss Fawdale?"

"Of course! The woman's presence was an insult! I wonder that my cousin stood it as long as she did!"

"You really think that Lady Stanmore's charges against her husband in relation to Miss Fawdale are true?"

"From all I have heard, and seen, I should say they are quite true! The thing was—obvious!"

"Well," said Charlesworth, after a moment's reflection. "Can I see Lady Stanmore for a few minutes? And will you be present, doctor? The fact is, I found something—a document—in Sir Charles Stanmore's clothing this afternoon which I should like her to see. There's nothing to upset her in it—she probably knows all about it."

Beck fetched Lady Stanmore to the waiting-room. Charlesworth noticed at once that she had made no pretence of wearing mourning; on the contrary she was very smartly dressed and looked in much better health and spirits than when he had last seen her; she was more gracious, too, in manner, and he wondered why Stanmore had not got on with her.

"I have something that I want to show you, Lady Stanmore," he said, as she took the chair he drew forward for her. "I examined certain articles of Sir Charles Stanmore's clothing to-day, and in the inner pocket of a leather under-jacket which he wore when motoring and had on, I am told, the night he returned from town, just previous to his death, I found—this! The envelope, you see, is addressed to your ladyship; so is the enclosed letter. And I want to know if you have seen both before?"

Lady Stanmore did no more than glance at the letter and envelope which Charlesworth laid on the table before her and Dr. Beck.

"Oh, yes!" she exclaimed, "of course I have! The letter came to the Manor by the last post that evening."

"You read it?"

"I read it—of course!"

"What did you think about it?"

"Oh, I don't know—it only told me what I already knew!"

"Knew?—or surmised?" asked Charlesworth.

"Well, some of it I knew; some of it I'd a pretty good idea of."

"What did you do with this letter, Lady Stanmore?"

"I took it into Sir Charles' study. There were letters awaiting him, on his desk. I slipped this amongst them."

"You wanted him to see it?"

"Certainly! That's why I put it there."

"What was your object?"

"Oh, I don't know—exactly! Perhaps to let him see that he was being found out. Perhaps to show him that I knew he was being found out. And—perhaps to vex him! He'd vexed me quite enough!"

"Any further intentions, Lady Stanmore?"

Lady Stanmore played with the rings on her fingers for a moment.

"Oh, well!" she replied, after a pause. "Yes! My intention was to leave the house next morning, at a very early hour, and never to enter it again."

"You saw nothing of Sir Charles that night?"

"Nothing!"

"Nor heard anything?"

"Nor heard anything!"

"No one appears to have seen Sir Charles that night," remarked Charlesworth. "Odd!—in such a big house, with so many people in it!" He waited a moment, and then went off on another tack. "There's a question I would like to ask you, Lady Stanmore," he continued. "You've heard, I suppose, all about this diamond necklace of Lady Verringham's, which Sir Charles had in his possession, and is now missing? Well—did you yourself ever see it?"

"Yes!" replied Lady Stanmore. "I did!"

"When?"

"The day preceding that of which we've been talking. He came home from town earlier that day—he dined at home. Mrs. John Stanmore and I were in the drawing-room just before dinner—he came in there, took the necklace out of his pocket, and showed it to both of us."

"Did he tell you what it was worth?"

"I think he said something about twenty-five or thirty thousand pounds. Mrs. John Stanmore was horrified to think of his carrying it about in his pocket."

"Do you know, Lady Stanmore, if he showed it to any other person—in the house?"

Lady Stanmore frowned. An unmistakably vindictive look came into her eyes.

"You may be quite certain he showed it to his so-called secretary!" she answered, with a palpable sneer. "That goes without saying!"

"You didn't see him show it to her, though?" suggested Charlesworth.

Lady Stanmore turned and stared at him.

"I?" she exclaimed. "Do you think I would enter or remain in any room where that woman was? No!"

Charlesworth made his bow, and went away. Looking at his watch outside, he found that it was scarcely half-past four, so he jumped into a taxi-cab and went off to Gilford's office. And closeted with Gilford he told him of his discovery, and of his interview with Lady Stanmore.

"From what Beck told me, I feel sure there was nothing between him and Lady Stanmore," he said in conclusion, "but it's very evident that Lady Stanmore is absolutely convinced that there was a long-standing liaison between her husband and Miss Fawdale. She's singularly outspoken about it, too!"

"Perhaps rather too much so!" remarked Gilford. He remained silent a moment, and then picked up a letter from amongst the papers on his desk. "Now!" he said. "I may as well tell you about this, Charlesworth, in view of what you've just told me. You see this?—it's a letter which arrived this morning, from Miss Fawdale's solicitors!"

"Oh?" said Charlesworth. "And—what about?"

"It's a very nasty letter," replied Gilford. "Pretty lengthy, too. I'll tell you the gist of it. They say that their client, Miss Irene Fawdale, has consulted them as regards certain charges brought against her by Lady Stanmore, at Aldersyke Manor the other day, in the presence of various people, who are named, yourself amongst them. Lady Stanmore, they are informed, on this occasion told those people that Miss Fawdale——"

"Miss Fawdale wasn't present," interrupted Charlesworth.

"No doubt—I suppose Mrs. John Stanmore, or Bedford, or possibly Superintendent Harding, told her what had passed. Anyway—told these people that she, Miss Fawdale, had been for some time and was still Sir Charles Stanmore's mistress: an explicit charge, which, they are informed, Lady Stanmore said she could substantiate. Well, the letter goes on to say that they are instructed by their client to write to me, as the late Sir Charles' partner, executor, trustee, and so forth, to give a most emphatic denial to this charge, in which, says Miss Fawdale, there is not one particle of truth. Miss Fawdale further wishes them to say that she, at a very early age, was left in charge of Sir Charles Stanmore by her father when he died, her mother already being dead, and that Sir Charles had always treated her as his ward. She indignantly denies the aspersions on her character, and as Lady Stanmore made these charges in public, she demands an equally public withdrawal of them. Otherwise—eh?"

"Otherwise what?" asked Charlesworth.

Gilford folded up the letter and tossed it into an open drawer.

"Action for slander, I suppose," he said. "Great mistake on Lady Stanmore's part to say what she did! I suppose nobody knows the real truth except Sir Charles—and he's dead—and this girl. And of course, if it were true, she wouldn't admit it!"

"I wish I could get at some explanation of that will business!" said Charlesworth. "What *had* happened to make Stanmore resolve on making such a difference——"

Just then a clerk put his head into Gilford's room and looked at Charlesworth.

"Beg pardon, sir," he said, turning to his employer, "Mr. Bedford is 'phoning from Aldersyke Manor to ask if Mr. Charlesworth is here—he'd been trying to get him at Headquarters and they replied he might be here. Mr. Bedford says if Mr. Charlesworth is here, will he please return to the Manor at once?"

Charlesworth went immediately, in the first taxi that came to hand—wondering all the way why the butler had summoned him so hurriedly.

CHAPTER XIV
THE SCRAP OF PAPER

Bedford was on the look-out for Charlesworth's arrival, and as soon as the detective reached the Manor led him into his pantry and closed the door on himself and his visitor with an air of confidential import.

"I've got something for you, Mr. Charlesworth!" he whispered, ignoring the fact that they were safe within four thick walls. "Something that I think will throw a bit of light on certain dark passages, sir! That's why I sent for you in a hurry—I thought you ought to know it at once."

"Much obliged to you, Bedford," said Charlesworth. "Glad of anything in the way of illumination! And—what is it?"

"Just this, Mr. Charlesworth. There's a girl in this house, Susan Carter—Susie, we call her—a housemaid, who knows something! As a matter of fact, she's told me, in confidence, what it is. She came to me to-day, asking if she could have a word with me in private. Of course, I assented—never dreaming what it was. Then, she told me. She'll tell you—but she's shy; shy, Mr. Charlesworth. A simple, country girl, you understand?—and that sort is always afraid of saying anything. Suspicious of getting themselves into trouble, you know. But all they want is encouraging to speak out. And, of course, she's frightened of having anything to do with police or detectives."

"No need to be afraid of me, I think, Bedford," laughed Charlesworth. "But—is it something important?"

"It's about something she saw with her own eyes, sir, that night Sir Charles came by his death," replied Bedford. "I should say—highly important. But I'll fetch her in, Mr. Charlesworth—you'll know how to talk to her."

He went away and presently returned with a good-looking, rosy-cheeked girl, who glanced shyly at Charlesworth and was obviously nervous about speaking to him. Charlesworth smiled, and rising from his seat, set a chair for her.

"This Susan Carter?" he asked. "Well, Susan, I hear you've got something to tell me?—something you've already told to Mr. Bedford. What is it, now?"

The housemaid took the chair offered her and fingered her apron.

"I don't want to get anybody into trouble," she said, repeating a formula which Charlesworth remembered to have heard a hundred times from diffident witnesses. "All the same, I felt I ought to tell somebody."

"Quite right," said Charlesworth. "Very proper! If you know anything, it's your duty to tell. And you can be quite comfortable in your mind about it—it'll go no further, at present, and if it ever does go further, I'll see that you're all right. So—what is it you can tell?"

The girl hesitated a moment, looking doubtfully from one man to the other. Bedford gave her an encouraging nod.

"Go on, Susie!" he said. "It's all right—quite all right."

"Well, it's about that night that there's been so much talk about in the house," began the girl. "The night that Sir Charles died—when, of course, they're all saying he was poisoned. It's about something I saw that night."

"Yes—and what did you see?" asked Charlesworth.

"Well, it was some time after I'd gone to bed. It would be more than two hours after—in fact, I know what time it was, because we've an alarum clock in our room, and I looked at the time; it was a bit after twelve. I had an awful attack of face-ache, just then, and I couldn't sleep for it, and at last I got up to go down to the kitchens to make a pepper-plaster to put on the place. And I went down and made one. It was as I was going back to my room that I saw what I told Mr. Bedford about."

"Yes?—and what was it?" asked Charlesworth, encouragingly.

"Well, it was this. I was just going up the second flight of stairs on the back staircase when I heard a door opened, very quietly. I knew what door it was. It was a door in a side-passage; you can get out into the gardens through that door. I heard it closed again, softly, and a key turned. Then I heard somebody coming along the passage, walking very gentle. So I stood still and looked over the banisters into the hall, down below. There's two halls—this one I was looking into opens into the big hall. There's always a light left burning there all night. I saw a figure come out of the passage, cross the first hall, and open the door of the front hall. Then, when it got into the light I saw who it was."

"Well?" said Charlesworth. "And who was it?"

The girl hesitated; it was obvious that she had all the thoroughgoing rustic's dread of mentioning names.

"Well," she faltered at last, "I shouldn't say so, if I wasn't sure about it. But I am sure about it! It was Miss Fawdale!"

"Yes?" said Charlesworth, as if indifferently. "And what did Miss Fawdale do?"

"She went into the front hall. After a minute or so she came back and went along the corridor towards the master's study. But she was back at once, and she went into the front hall again and shut the door, and of course I didn't see any more. I went up to my room then."

"Anybody share your room with you?" asked Charlesworth.

"Yes—Annie Marshall, another housemaid."

"Was she awake when you went back?"

"No—she was asleep."

"Did you tell her next morning of what you'd seen?"

"No, I didn't. I might have done, but you see, there was so much talk in the kitchens about Sir Charles that I thought I'd better keep my tongue still."

"So you never mentioned this to anybody until you told Mr. Bedford this morning?"

"No!"

Charlesworth nodded and rose from his chair.

"Just come and show me where you were standing when you saw Miss Fawdale," he said. "And where she was standing. Come with us, Bedford."

Susan Carter led the two men to the back staircase and indicated the exact place in which she had stood, and Charlesworth, placing himself there, became satisfied as to the practicability of seeing into the two halls below. He dismissed Susan Carter with an assurance of safety for herself and an admonition to hold her tongue, and telling Bedford that he was going to have a look at the side-door and then at the gardens outside, got rid of the butler. About the side-door he was quickly satisfied: it stood at the end of a narrow passage leading from the second of the two halls, and admitted to the gardens at the side of the house. Passing through these, Charlesworth turned his attention to the shrubbery. He had no doubt whatever, after hearing Susan Carter's story, that the woman seen in company with a man by Mappleson after leaving Sir Charles Stanmore that night was Miss Fawdale. But—who was her companion? And what was the object of their midnight meeting? And—far more important!—had it any relation to Sir Charles Stanmore's death?

Once out in the grounds, and alone, Charlesworth began a careful examination of his surroundings. The door through which he had passed and by which, according to Susan Carter, Miss Fawdale had entered the house, gave access first of all to a corner of the kitchen gardens, and thence, through an opening in a holly hedge, to the ornamental grounds beyond. There was plenty of cover everywhere: Charlesworth saw at once how easily anyone could slip out of the house and pass unobserved towards the belt of high trees and the undergrowth of thick shrubbery which effectually shut off the Manor from the high road beyond. He went through gardens and grounds towards the carriage drive, noting the position of the window in Sir Charles Stanmore's study by which Mappleson had said he left the house. From that window it was but a few steps, across a smooth lawn, to the carriage drive. The carriage drive twisted a good deal; there was more smooth lawn on each side of it; Charlesworth saw that any person walking along this velvet-like verge would not be likely to be heard until he was close upon anyone happening to be about. He concluded, from his observations, that it was at a particular point of the carriage drive where it made a sharp turn towards the lodge-gates that Mappleson had seen the two figures he described. They had vanished at his approach into the shrubbery, he said; Charlesworth turned into the shrubbery. It seemed a futile thing to do, but you never knew, after all, what luck you might have in these matters. And he had luck, for he had scarcely plunged in amongst the laurels and rhododendrons when, in a bit of open ground, he saw, lying before him, a silver cigarette case.

To possess himself of this, to snap it open, and to see what was inside, was the work of a second. There were half a dozen cigarettes of an expensive brand on one side of the case, and on the other was a folded scrap of paper. Charlesworth unfolded it eagerly, and saw two lines of writing, a woman's writing, in pencil, obviously hastily scribbled:—

"*Be sure to come to-night: usual time and place—most important.*"

He re-folded the scrap of paper, returned it to its place, and closing the cigarette case, inspected its exterior, hoping to find a monogram, or initials, anything that could give a clue to its ownership. But the case, a solid silver and evidently expensive one, was perfectly plain as to its exterior; there was nothing whatever on it to show to whom it belonged. And putting it safely away in his pocket, Charlesworth returned to the house, and finding Bedford in his pantry, shut the door, and after pledging the butler to secrecy, told and showed him what he had found.

"Now do you know whose case this is, Bedford?" he asked. "Have you ever seen it before?"

But Bedford's shake of the head was decisive.

"No, sir, no, can't say that I have!" he answered. "Many like it, or something like it—perfectly plain silver, you see, sir. Cost a bit, did that case, though, Mr. Charlesworth, and it's odd that it hasn't a monogram on it. Not being a present, that, sir—whoever bought it, bought it for himself and didn't bother about having it engraved. No, sir, can't say I know it—but as regards that handwriting, Mr. Charlesworth, I know that—and well enough! It's Miss Fawdale's!"

"Certain?" demanded Charlesworth. "Positive?"

"As certain as I am that I see you, sir! I know Miss Fawdale's writing well enough. That's it!"

Charlesworth put the scrap of paper and the cigarette case safely away again. He was convinced now beyond all doubt that Miss Fawdale was the woman whom Mappleson had seen in company with a man. And having taken Bedford into his confidence already about a good many things, he took him into it still more and repeated Mappleson's story to him.

"Doesn't seem to be much doubt about that, sir," remarked Bedford, lifting his eyebrows expressively. "That's been Miss F. sure enough! Very mysterious, I think, Mr. Charlesworth. Now who could the gentleman be? For between you and me and the wall, sir, as the saying is, I never knew Miss F. show what you'd call any partiality for gentlemen!"

"Never heard of anything of that sort with any young men of the neighbourhood, eh?" suggested Charlesworth.

"Never, sir! I should have said that Miss F.—from what I saw of her—was not, as I say, partial to gentlemen. Not that sort at all, sir—from my observation of the young lady."

"What sort was she, now?" asked Charlesworth.

"Odd, sir, very odd! Never could make her out, nor her relation to Sir Charles, nor—nor anything!" declared Bedford. "Masterful, sir, very—and always took care to get her own way about everything. Never knew a young woman in my life who just calmly did whatever she liked—and if she was in any way balked of what she wanted, got it just the same. Do you know, sir," continued Bedford, waxing eloquent, "I've known Sir Charles forbid, actually forbid, Miss F. to do a thing; forbid her, sir, in my presence, and angrily, too. And—she'd just stare at him as innocent as a child might look, sir, and—do it before his eyes!"

"And—what did he do, then?" asked Charlesworth.

"Do, sir? Why, he'd swear first—and laugh afterwards," replied the butler. "Oh—she'd a deal of power, that young lady. Lady Stanmore, sir," he continued, sinking his voice to a whisper, "between you and me, she was a cypher in this house, till she turned Miss F.

out. And do you know, Mr. Charlesworth, since we are talking about Miss F., I'll tell you of something that's puzzled me, greatly. You remember that I was instructed, in your presence, to dismiss Miss F., there and then? Well, sir, do you know that when I saw her in her rooms, she already had all her trunks and belongings packed ready to go! She was going, there and then, evidently—without any dismissal! Now, why?"

"She had her reasons, no doubt," said Charlesworth. "And that reminds me—when Superintendent Harding and I were leaving the house that morning we came across the new baronet and Miss Fawdale talking at the lodge-gates. He seemed to be in a bad temper. How did he and Miss Fawdale get on, Bedford?—he used to come here, didn't he?"

"Now and then, sir—not a great deal," replied Bedford. "Well, sir, I don't think they got on at all well! My opinion, sir, is that Miss F. was jealous of Mr. Guy Stanmore—she couldn't bear, you know, sir, to see Sir Charles favour anybody but herself. Yes, I'm sure she was always jealous of Mr. Guy—I've seen her show it. Odd young woman, sir!—she'd got to be first, or there was unpleasantness."

Charlesworth went away after that, and on thinking things over carried the result of his various inquiries to his superiors at Headquarters.

CHAPTER XV
THE PLAY BOX

The all-important Personage to whom Charlesworth was in the habit of making his reports and from whom he took his orders was a man of few words; he listened much and said little. And when Charlesworth, as succinctly as possible, but still at some length, had unbosomed himself of the story of his investigations and discoveries, the great man's orders came sharp and pat.

"Find out everything you can about this woman Fawdale's antecedents, and about her relations, business or otherwise, with Sir Charles Stanmore, and report to me!" he commanded. "Get on to it at once!"

Charlesworth went off—to get on to it. It was just about time for his lunch when he received these marching orders, and he turned into a quiet hostelry that he knew of and picking out a seat in a corner began, as he ate and drank, to consider seriously what he was after. When he had got thinking he had to confess to himself that up to that point he had had no very clear ideas. But he had a quantity of that very useful commodity called Fact. It was a fact (for the medical men had by this time supplied definite information on the point) that Sir Charles Stanmore had been poisoned, and it was practically certain that the poison had not been self-administered; in other words, this was not a case of suicide but of murder. It had also been established by the medical men that the poison, a most subtle one, had been taken from a particular bottle in the Borgia Cabinet. All that made Fact number One—Murder. Well, Fact number Two was that at the time of his murder, Sir Charles Stanmore was in possession of Lady Verringham's diamond necklace, worth say thirty thousand pounds, and that it had disappeared. Fact number Three was that a copy of Sir Charles Stanmore's will was lying about on his desk for anybody to read, and that there were provisions in that will of a nature highly gratifying to several beneficiaries: it was impossible to read that will without seeing how considerably several people would benefit whenever Sir Charles Stanmore departed this life. Lady Stanmore (especially considering that she loathed her husband) would be much better off. Mrs. John Stanmore would be much better off. Miss

Irene Fawdale would be much better off. Bedford the butler would be much better off. Even Purser the housemaid would be better off. And . . . any one of these people had the means, and the opportunity, and every facility for ridding the world of Sir Charles Stanmore, for according to Charlesworth's knowledge they all knew of the existence of the Borgia Cabinet and were aware of the nature of its contents—some of them knew, too, that there were poisons in that cabinet the exact nature of which were utterly unknown to British medical or chemical authorities, if Lady Stanmore's father's book on the subject was to be trusted. And there was also Guy Stanmore—the quiet removal of his uncle would place that young gentleman in the enviable position of not only succeeding to a baronetcy but to a fortune of some eight or nine hundred thousand pounds.

But Charlesworth didn't and couldn't believe that any one of these people had poisoned Sir Charles Stanmore. Lady Stanmore wanted to be free—but she was going to seek her freedom in a court of law. Mrs. John Stanmore didn't seem the sort of person who would poison a man for the sake of twenty-five thousand pounds. Nor did Bedford, for the sake of a handsome legacy. Nor did Purser—for the sake of a very nice one. As to Guy Stanmore, Charlesworth had no suspicion whatever—he left Guy Stanmore clean out of all reckonings. Well, there remained Miss Fawdale. What did, what could he make of her?

There were no end of queer things about Miss Fawdale, he reflected, as he ate and drank in his lonely corner. Who was she?—and what, exactly, were her relations with Sir Charles Stanmore? What was the cause and the nature of the row, quarrel, disagreement with him which Bedford overheard the morning before Sir Charles Stanmore's sudden death? Was it in consequence of that that she had her trunks packed ready next day?—was she going to clear out, whether Sir Charles Stanmore was alive or dead, because of that row? And why was she in the grounds of Aldersyke Manor and hiding in a shrubbery with a man at midnight, that very night on which her employer met his death? Queer, all of it!

But there was something queerer, something that needed a lot of clearing up. In Sir Charles Stanmore's will, the will which Gilford possessed and declared nothing could upset, Miss Irene Fawdale was remembered handsomely, generously, and Guy Stanmore (certainly, *he* came in at this!) was left the residue of his uncle's estate. Why, only a few days before his death, had Sir Charles Stanmore gone to a brother solicitor privately and given him instructions for a new will in which Miss Fawdale and Guy Stanmore were left just enough to put bread and cheese in their mouths for life—and no more? What—now *what* was the reason? *What?*

"Same old game!" mused Charlesworth as he finished his lunch and lighted his pipe. "Always is! There's a secret somewhere—and somebody knows it! And, as usual, the somebody's keeping it to himself or herself! No use theorizing—I've got to dig down, and go back, and rake up!" Then he became solemnly epigrammatic. "Solutions of present mysteries lie in past histories!" he said to himself. "Sounds like poetry! Well—where to begin?"

He knew where not to begin. It was no use going to Miss Irene Fawdale herself. Her solicitors had been approached by Gilford in relation to the letter which Gilford had shown to Charlesworth, and they had behaved in a very cavalier fashion. Miss Fawdale, they said, would be produced by them at the proper moment, to wit, at the adjourned inquest, or, they maliciously added, at any police-court proceedings which might eventuate; until then she was not to be annoyed. As to her address, that was her own business, and theirs. But Bedford knew Miss Fawdale's address in London, and Charlesworth had set a brother-detective to find out if she was still at it. She was not—inquiries showed that she had given up her flat and gone away. Taxed with this, her solicitors had replied scornfully that they were quite aware of their client's movements and had repeated their intention of producing her—at the right time and place, and this with a hint that her appearance in a witness-box might have some very unpleasant consequences for—somebody.

But there must be a beginning of this quest—and to get at one he turned once more to Aldersyke Manor and to its butler. Bedford, so far, had been of inestimable use; he might be still more useful.

"Here I am again, you see, Bedford!" he exclaimed, once again installed in the butler's pantry over a cup of tea that afternoon. "And again fishing for information! Can't get going without it, you know."

"What is it this time, Mr. Charlesworth?" asked Bedford. "Anything that I can tell, sir——"

"You'll be glad to tell, of course," laughed Charlesworth. "Well, it's pretty much the same old thing. I want to know more about Miss Fawdale."

"Yes, sir? And in what direction, Mr. Charlesworth?"

"Backward! I want to go back, perhaps further back than you can take me. But to start with—and of course, Bedford, all this is between you and me!—do you remember when she first came here?"

"Very well indeed, sir!—as well as if it were yesterday!"

"It's—how long ago?"

"About nine years, sir."

"How old was she, then?"

"I should say, sir, between eighteen and nineteen years of age. That, sir, is my estimate. She might have been a bit younger, or a bit older. A well-grown young lady, Mr. Charlesworth."

"Sir Charles Stanmore brought her, I suppose?"

"She came here with him, sir—certainly!"

"Well," said Charlesworth, "to come to the precise point—what I want to know is, do you know where she came from?"

But Bedford shook his head.

"Haven't the least idea, Mr. Charlesworth—not the very least! Of course, she came with Sir Charles from London, one day—I remember it very well. But—that's nothing, is it?"

"Nothing! What I want to get at is, where had she been, lived, and so on, before that. You don't know—anything?"

"Nothing at all, sir! She came, as I say, with Sir Charles, in his car, one afternoon, and settled down here—she was given a suite of rooms. The flat in London wasn't started until after Sir Charles's marriage."

"Well, I suppose she brought some belongings with her?" suggested Charlesworth. "Have you any recollection of what she brought?"

Bedford's expression brightened.

"I have, sir! She brought—or, rather, there came immediately after her arrival, a considerable amount of luggage. Most of it was new—I formed the opinion that the young lady had been getting a regular outfit in town: I certainly noticed—I've a bit of a noticing eye, Mr. Charlesworth—that most of her gowns were brand new, and a nice penny they must have cost, too!"

"Notice any other things?" asked Charlesworth. "Think!—of anything."

Bedford replenished his tea-cup, and proceeded to reflect over its rim.

"Things come back, of course," he said, meditatively, "when one turns one's mind that way. Yes—there's one matter I recollect, very well indeed. When Miss F. first came here, I thought she was French."

"French? Why?"

"Well, her English wasn't over good, Mr. Charlesworth. She spoke English, of course, but nothing like as easily as she spoke French. She and Sir Charles Stanmore, sir, always did their talking in French—they kept that up to the end, for he spoke French like a native. That, sir, was one of the things that vexed and angered Lady Stanmore so, for she spoke no French. Yes, I certainly thought Miss Fawdale was a Frenchwoman when she first came."

"Perhaps she was," said Charlesworth. "But I wish I knew where she came from when she did come!"

"And that I can't say anything about, sir," replied Bedford. "But I'll tell you what, Mr. Charlesworth—in one of our box-rooms there's a small box, a wooden box, sir, which was amongst the other things that Miss F. brought with her, at her first coming. It was put up there when she came, and she's never asked for it since and she left it behind her when she went away the other day: I should say she's completely forgotten its existence! Just a plain wooden box, sir; Mr. Guy had a similar one when he was at school, Mr. Charlesworth—his was termed a play-box."

Charlesworth jumped from his chair.

"Good!" he exclaimed. "Can I see it? Is it unlocked?—can one examine its contents?"

"I can't say if it's unlocked or not, sir," replied Bedford. "I only know that it's there—I should say it's never been touched since it was carried up to that room. Come this way, Mr. Charlesworth."

Charlesworth followed the butler to the upper regions of the big house, and in a room filled with old trunks, portmanteaux, suit-cases and odds and ends of travelling appliances, found himself confronting a plain wooden chest on which were painted the initials I.F.

"That's a play-box, all right!" he muttered. "I suppose girls have 'em as well as boys. Locked! Um!—well, Bedford, I'm going to have a look inside. And I shan't break the lock, either!"

Giving the butler a knowing wink, Charlesworth produced from his pocket what looked to Bedford like a bit of bent steel. Inserting it in the lock he gave it a twist or two and a second later turned back the lid.

"Present from an accomplished cracksman, that, Bedford!" he said laughing, as he put the pick-lock back in his pocket. "And highly useful on occasions such as these. Well, here we are!" he went on, turning back a fold of faded newspapers. "What have we—dolls? No—school-books—exercise books. But by gad! Bedford!—here's a clue, the very thing I'm wanting. See, man! *Irene Fawdale, Rithendene School*!—there it is, written again and again, in exercise books, and school-books! Splendid. But Rithendene? Where's Rithendene?"

"I can inform you as to that, sir," replied Bedford, promptly. "Rithendene School is one of the best—and I believe, sir, one of the most expensive schools for young ladies in England. One of my previous employers, Lord Medderdale, sent his two daughters there—a very fine establishment, I'm given to understand, sir. Dear me!—I'd no idea that Miss F. had been there!"

"But where is it?" asked Charlesworth, busily turning over the contents of the box, and finding nothing but school and exercise books. "How do you get to it?"

"The nearest station, sir, is Shelhampton, on the Southern Railway," replied Bedford. "Rithendene, sir, is a village on the coast—a most salubrious situation, according to the advertisements."

"Well, Miss Fawdale, evidently, was educated there," remarked Charlesworth, as he turned over the contents of the box. "There's no doubt about that. And I suppose the authorities there will know something about her. Anyway . . ." He said no more, however, on that point. Closing the box and restoring it to its niche in the alcove from which he had pulled it out, he left the box-room and presently bade Bedford farewell.

"I shall no doubt have something to tell you next time I turn up here," he said, with a smile. "In the meantime, keep your eyes and ears open!"

Then he went away, more hopeful than when he arrived. For he had got at least the first beginnings of a clue . . . and first beginnings mean a good deal.

CHAPTER XVI
TURNING BACKWARD

Charlesworth found himself next day prospecting the one winding street of a coast village in which, set high above sea and land, was but one building of any significance—a great house of extent and grandeur enough to resemble a mediæval castle, or, perhaps, the buildings of some important ecclesiastical foundation. A single inquiry made him acquainted with the fact that this was Rithendene School: its very size and consequence rather frightened him. Probably there were hundreds of girls there; had been thousands in past years; how was he going to recover news of one? And how, too, to find anybody who could give him news of that particular one? To consider this, and to glean a little information about the place he had come to see, he turned into the village inn, and over a crust of bread and cheese and a glass of ale, extracted some facts from the landlord. Yes, to be sure the school was *the* feature of that part of the world; there were those who did say that it was the finest school for young ladies in England, not to speak of foreign parts. Rare lot of money it did cost, to be sure, to send a young lady there—he, the landlord, had heard it said as how three to four hundred pounds a year was the figure. Five hundred girls there were there—and from their looks, the pick of the nation, sure-ly! Governesses and mistresses?—Lor bless you, they reckoned them by the dozens, and servants by the score—no expense of any sort spared up there, you may be sure! Some of the young ladies had their own riding-horses, and there wasn't a game under the sun that they didn't play at—oh, proper nobs they were at Rithendene, he could vouch for it. Who was what you'd call the boss lady of the show?—eh, that, to be sure, was Miss Torrance—very grand lady indeed, Miss Torrance, and about as easy to get at as the Pope his-self. There, yes!—but he didn't know as he knew anybody in the village as had ever been privileged to see her—enough to do, no doubt, to manage such a big establishment.

Charlesworth nerved himself to the task of seeing or endeavouring to see Miss Torrance and made his way through plantations of pine and larch to the great buildings on the hillside. He was soon lost in a maze of quadrangles, courts, and what not, but eventually a friendly gardener showed him the way to the head-mistress' lodge. And there, upon reflection, he sent in to Miss Torrance, enclosed in an envelope, his official card. He had an idea that this would gain him an audience, and he was not mistaken. Within a few minutes he was shown into a waiting-room and told that Miss Torrance would come to him—and almost at once Miss Torrance came.

Charlesworth inspected Miss Torrance with deep interest: it seemed to him that any woman who could run an establishment of that size and extent must be a truly remarkable specimen of her sex. And in expecting to see something remarkable, Charlesworth was not disappointed. Miss Torrance was one of those women who in certain circumstances become heads of great religious communities, and in others of big businesses, and in still others, of vast movements: she was the type that controls, organizes, rules. But Charlesworth saw that she was approachable.

"You have read, of course, Miss Torrance, of the mysterious death of Sir Charles Stanmore, of Aldersyke Manor, recently?" he asked when he had apologized for calling without an appointment. "I am engaged in attempting to clear up the mystery, and from certain information that has come into my hands, I believe that you can give me some assistance. May I ask a direct question? Did you ever know Sir Charles Stanmore?"

Miss Torrance, who had been inspecting her visitor with an air of interest, bowed her head at once.

"Yes!" she answered. "Quite well, at one time. I knew him as the guardian of a girl we had here for four or five years—Irene Fawdale."

"Your reply simplifies matters a good deal, Miss Torrance," said Charlesworth. "You perhaps saw that Miss Fawdale's name occurred in the newspaper accounts of Sir Charles Stanmore's death?"

"I saw that she was referred to as Sir Charles' secretary," replied Miss Torrance. She smiled a little. "I was rather surprised at that!"

"Why, may I ask?" inquired Charlesworth.

"From my recollection of her, and my knowledge of her acquirements, I shouldn't have thought Irene Fawdale capable of discharging the duties of secretary to anyone!" answered Miss Torrance, still smiling.

"Not—accomplished enough?" suggested Charlesworth. "Not clever enough?"

"Oh, she was clever enough! But—well, that is my impression. I don't exactly identify her with what one means when one uses the word secretary. Perhaps she developed secretarial qualities after leaving me."

"I am particularly anxious to get all the information I can about Miss Fawdale," said Charlesworth. "It—it is necessary. Anything you can tell me will be treated as a confidential communication, Miss Torrance. To begin with, was she placed at your school by Sir Charles Stanmore?"

"Yes—oh, yes. Sir Charles Stanmore came to me some little time before he brought her here and made all the necessary arrangements."

"Did he tell you who she was?"

"Yes. He said she was his ward. Her father and mother were dead. The father, I understood, had died either before she was born or soon after; the mother, too, had not long survived Irene's birth. I forget the exact details, but that is the impression I have. The father and mother had been friends of Sir Charles Stanmore, and he had charged himself with the care of the child."

"And I suppose he paid the cost of her education here?"

"Oh, yes! My recollection is that he spent a great deal of money on her. She had everything she wanted—that is, everything she was permitted to have, here. In the holidays I should say she had a great deal more than any girl of that age ought to have. But I had nothing to do with that—she spent her holidays with Sir Charles Stanmore."

"You think he spoilt her?"

"I am sure of it. I used to tell him so, but it had no effect. He came here to see her so often that I had to stop that. It was difficult—he struck me as being the sort of man who will have his own way."

"I'm given to understand that he was, Miss Torrance. I'm also told that Miss Fawdale is a good deal like that. Did you notice it?"

Miss Torrance turned the rings on her white fingers, looking sidewise at them. "Oh, well!" she replied. "If you really want to know what I thought of Irene Fawdale, especially as she grew older, I will tell you. She was a very masterful, self-opinionated, and in a certain degree, intensely selfish girl, who allowed nothing to come between her and her desires, if she could help it, and I think Sir Charles Stanmore, instead of trying to eradicate this side of her character, helped to develop it. I warned him of that, too, but he only laughed at me. From what little I saw of him, I think he was rather a strange man."

"He certainly did some strange things," agreed Charlesworth. "But Miss Torrance, there is another and a very important question that I want to ask you. You say that Miss Fawdale was here four or five years? I'm told that she was about eighteen or nineteen years of age when she first went to live at Aldersyke Manor, and that she went there from your school. So—she would be about fourteen when she came to you. But—where had she been before? Who, if her father and mother were dead, had brought her up? Do you know anything about that?"

"Yes," replied Miss Torrance, readily. "I do! Irene Fawdale, from three years old was entirely brought up by a clergyman and his wife, Mr. and Mrs. Penney. Mr. Penney is vicar of Chandow St. Martin, in Kent."

"Was she placed with them by Sir Charles Stanmore?" asked Charlesworth, "or were they relations?"

"That I do not know," said Miss Torrance. "All I know is that she had lived with them and been educated by them from a mere child of three until she came here. Sir Charles Stanmore told me that much himself; as for Irene, I never remember hearing her mention them."

"Odd, that, wasn't it, Miss Torrance?" suggested Charlesworth. "You'd have thought she'd have some recollections——"

"It wasn't odd—in her," interrupted Miss Torrance. "Irene Fawdale, during the time I knew her, showed herself to be an unusually self-centred young person. There was but one being in the world for her—herself!"

"I gather that you didn't like her?" said Charlesworth.

"Frankly, I didn't!" replied Miss Torrance, candidly. "Though I had no complaint to make as regards her conduct. She kept the rules of the school, and did her work, and there was nothing against her. But I formed my own opinion of her character and that was that she was selfish and egotistical to an unusual degree." She paused, with an inquisitive smile. "And now," she continued, "as I have told you all I know, tell me something, if you please. What is all this about? For you are, you tell me, a detective,—a detective—eh?"

"I told you that there is a great deal of mystery centring in Sir Charles Stanmore's death, Miss Torrance," replied Charlesworth. "According to the medical evidence he was poisoned—and there's nothing to show that he poisoned himself!"

"Then—murder?" questioned Miss Torrance.

"Something uncommonly like it!" said Charlesworth. "Yes—probably murder!"

"You don't surely suspect Irene Fawdale?" exclaimed Miss Torrance. "Her—benefactor!"

Charlesworth shrugged his shoulders.

"I don't know whom to suspect!" he answered. "There were two or three people in the house who could have poisoned Stanmore, but in each case there seems every reason why he or she shouldn't! It's got to be solved, however, and one thing helps another. As regards Miss Fawdale, I want to know who she is. Will you oblige me with Mr. Penney's full address, ma'am?—I must try him next."

He went away with the clergyman's address in his pocket and finding that Chandow St. Martin was easily accessible from his present whereabouts went on there by an afternoon train and towards evening presented himself at the vicarage door. And here after sending in his professional card he found as speedy admittance as at Rithendene and presently was in the presence of an elderly man who regarded him with even more curiosity than Miss Torrance had shown, and so far from being reticent at once betrayed an eagerness to talk which made Charlesworth wonder; Charlesworth, indeed, had no chance of asking questions before Mr. Penney began to ask them himself.

"Have you called on me in relation to this Sir Charles Stanmore case?" he asked, as he pointed his visitor to a chair. "I see you are of the detective force. Just so!—we have read a great deal about the case in the newspapers—most mysterious, and if I may say so, most interesting! And extremely interesting to my wife and myself, because we have seen Miss Irene Fawdale's name mentioned. Now Miss Fawdale, as a child, was in our care for some years!"

"So I have been given to understand, sir, and that is why I called on you," said Charlesworth. "I am doing all I can to clear up the mystery of this case, and I want to know all I can get to know about Miss Fawdale's antecedents——"

"You don't mean to say that you suspect *her*!" exclaimed Mr. Penney. "Dear, dear!—that would be a most terrible thing! Her guardian——"

"I can't say that Miss Fawdale is suspected, sir," interrupted Charlesworth. "But there is a mystery connected with the exact relations of Miss Fawdale with Sir Charles Stanmore which, if solved, may throw some light on the circumstances of his death. I hear—I heard, as a matter of fact, from Miss Torrance of Rithendene School—that Irene Fawdale lived several years in your house, as a child. That is so, I suppose?"

"That is so—quite right," assented Mr. Penney. "She was in our care from the time she was three years old until she was fourteen, when Sir Charles Stanmore removed her to Rithendene. I will tell you the circumstances. At the time Irene Fawdale came to us, my wife and I had one child—our only child, to be exact, for we have never had another—who was then nearly four years of age. We thought we should like our little daughter to have a companion of her own age; this, as you see, is a very lonely, out-of-the-way place, and there were no children in the village of whom she could make playmates. There was also—I am being very frank with you, because of your profession—a monetary consideration. This is not a rich living—far from it!—and I was not a rich man. We thought that if we could get a little girl to share our own little one's home and be educated with her by a first-class governess, it would be to the mutual advantage of—ourselves and whoever came into the arrangement. So we inserted an advertisement in *The Times*, saying what we wanted and what we offered. It was answered, almost at once, by Sir Charles Stanmore."

"In his own name?" inquired Charlesworth.

"Oh, certainly—in his own name! The letter, I remember, was written from his office in Lincoln's Inn Fields—I have a very good memory. Well, I replied to him, and he came down to see us. He told us that he was guardian of a little girl of three whose father and mother were both dead and that what we offered was exactly what he wanted for her. I may as well tell you that he was most generous about terms—as a matter of fact he increased the amount which we had named, saying that we were too modest, and that he wished the child to have every care and attention. We exchanged references, the matter was settled, and within a week or two Sir Charles brought Irene to us—to this house. She was then, as I say, three years old. Sir Charles had told us that her father and mother had died in France, and that she had spent the three years of her infancy in France. But we were no little surprised considering her English parentage to find, on her arrival, that the child did not know one word of English! She could only speak French!"

CHAPTER XVII
THE ROSEWOOD DESK

There was something in Mr. Penney's manner as he spoke these last words which attracted Charlesworth's attention, and he looked at his informant inquiringly.

"You seem to think that a curious circumstance, sir?" he said. "Now, as the child had been brought up in France, it seems to me a natural consequence. Probably she'd never heard English spoken."

"But—of English parentage?" replied Mr. Penney. "And we know that Sir Charles had visited her from time to time in France—why had he never talked English to her?"

"Most likely because he spoke French as well as he spoke English," said Charlesworth, smiling. "Reasonable explanation, I think, sir!"

"Well, well!" said Mr. Penney. "We thought it a very strange thing that a child born of English parents should know nothing of its own language! However, there was the fact. Irene did not know one word of English. But with her came a French nurse-maid, a superior sort of woman whom Sir Charles had engaged in Paris to look after the child. At his special request, and of course at his expense this woman remained here three years. Now there was another matter that we thought strange. This nurse, Aimée Forart, knew nothing whatever about the child's antecedents! All she knew was that a few days before Sir Charles Stanmore brought her and the child over to England he engaged her services in Paris, through an agency. He interviewed her at some fashionable hotel there, was very particular about her attainments and references, offered her what we considered almost absurdly high wages, and extracted a promise from her that she would remain with Irene in England for at least a year. As a matter of fact she remained three."

"Doing her duty, no doubt, sir?" suggested Charlesworth.

"She was certainly a very admirable servant," assented Mr. Penney in his simplest manner, "and, I am bound to say, relieved us of a great deal of responsibility: we were sorry when she left, for she was a woman of very good manners who spoke Parisian French perfectly, with a really cultured accent, and our own little girl learnt that language from her to such purpose that her French is, as one might say, that of a native. Oh, yes—this arrangement was a very good one."

"And, I suppose, while your little daughter was learning French from the nurse, Irene was learning English from the governess engaged by you and Mrs. Penney?" suggested Charlesworth.

"Ye-es!" replied Mr. Penney, dubiously. "Irene, of course, picked up English, but I am bound to say that, first, she was very slow in doing so, and second, she appeared to have a curious dislike to the language, and in fact, to anything English. We thought that odd, in view of the fact that her parentage was English. The truth is that the child, I suppose because she'd passed her first three years in France, seemed to be French to the core! It was difficult to think of her as English."

Charlesworth was beginning to grasp the worthy clergyman's limitations. But he wanted more information.

"Well, sir," he said, "Miss Irene Fawdale remained with you until she was fourteen years of age. She was growing up by that time. What was your impression of her character? What remains in your mind about her?"

Mr. Penney shook his head, sadly.

"I regret to say that as years passed on, Irene did not improve upon acquaintance," he said, with a mournful inflection. "She was a very wilful child, and her wilfulness increased rather than lessened. She was selfish, too—her selfishness, indeed, was her worst feature. And, I think, ungrateful. Of her ingratitude, I can give you a marked example. My wife, our daughter and myself always showed Irene the greatest kindness, and, as far as she would permit it, affection, all the time—eleven years, remember!—that she was with us. Yet, from the moment in which Sir Charles Stanmore removed her from our care and took her to that of Miss Torrance, she never wrote any one of us one letter or remembered us in any way! She was—I must use a quite new-fashioned term—self-centred."

Charlesworth made no comment on this; it was all of a piece, he reflected, with what he had already heard from Miss Torrance. He rose to go.

"So you know nothing whatever, sir, of Irene Fawdale's antecedents before she came to you?" he asked as a last question. "Nothing?"

"Nothing!" replied Mr. Penney.

"Nor from where in France she was brought to you?"

"Only that Sir Charles Stanmore brought her and the nurse, Aimée Forart, from Paris."

"Did the child never mention the name of any place she'd lived in?" suggested Charlesworth. "You say that Aimée Forart first saw her in a fashionable hotel in Paris. But whence had she come?"

"I cannot say!" replied Mr. Penney. "She may have spoken of some place she had known and of people she had known to her nurse, but you see neither Mrs. Penney nor myself speak the French language, so we shouldn't understand. No!—beyond what I have told you I know nothing."

Charlesworth returned to town, and next morning called on Gilford, to whom in confidence he communicated the result of his labours—so far.

"Um!" observed Gilford, cynically. "That, to me, sounds like the first chapter of a queer story! But you know I never knew Stanmore as a young man. Never knew him—personally, I mean—at all until I entered into partnership with him twenty years ago. There's one thing strikes me, however, about this story of yours, Charlesworth. According to what Stanmore told these people you've been interviewing, this girl, Irene, was the orphan daughter of one Fawdale and his wife. Now the other day, being a bit curious about certain things, I turned up Stanmore's record in the Baronetage—he was the second baronet, you know; his father got the baronetcy for some civic business or other, I forget what—and I found out that Stanmore's mother, the first Lady Stanmore, was a Miss Fawdale. Here you are," he continued, reaching across his desk for a portly volume. "There it is! His mother, you see, was Georgina Fawdale, only daughter of Samuel Fawdale, of Climpingwell Park, Dorsetshire. So—no doubt this girl is, as he made out, some relation, of whom he was left in charge."

"Why all the subsequent mystery about her?" asked Charlesworth. "I'm quite sure of this—neither the present Lady Stanmore, nor Mrs. John Stanmore, nor Bedford, the butler, know of her as a relation. To them she's been simply Miss Fawdale, the secretary—and we know what Lady Stanmore hints at!"

"Stanmore was a queer chap!" observed Gilford. "If he wanted to keep his mouth shut I don't know of any man who could do it better. But are you going on with this investigation?—and if so, what do you propose next?"

"I'm certainly going on with it," replied Charlesworth. "Got to—orders! Do?—well, I've been wondering if you have any private papers and that sort of thing of Stanmore's, here at your offices? If so——"

"You can come up to his private room and look," replied Gilford. "I don't know what there may be. I'll go up with you."

He led the way upstairs to a front room, the windows of which overlooked the square and gardens of the Fields; its blinds were drawn, and as he pulled them up Gilford glanced at his companion with a knowing look.

"Doesn't look much like a lawyer's den, does it?" he said, cynically. "As a matter of fact, Stanmore scarcely ever saw anybody but personal friends and very old clients here. He kept it as a private room for himself. But then, you know, of late years he had as little to do with the practice as he could help—he left most of it to me, as junior partner, and to our managing clerks. Certainly he spent a lot of time in this room—chiefly reading."

Gilford waved his hand as he spoke towards a fine old book-case which filled nearly the whole side of one wall, and Charlesworth, inspecting its contents, was quick to note that in addition to a fine selection of standard English works and a goodly representation of the classics there were two or three shelves entirely filled with French books, all in characteristically French bindings. He noticed, too, on looking round the walls that Stanmore had evidently possessed a discerning taste in French pictures. Most of them were modern, but there was a genuine Corot over the mantelpiece, and an undeniable Daubigny on the wall opposite Stanmore's writing-table. There were other things in the room which showed that its late occupant had been a man of taste—but there were no lawbooks on the shelves and no bundles of papers tied up with pink tape on the table.

"Just as he left it, this room, I suppose?" suggested Charlesworth.

"Exactly! Nobody's touched it," said Gilford.

"Has Lady Stanmore been in it—since he died?" asked Charlesworth.

"Lady Stanmore? Good Lord, no!" exclaimed Gilford. "I never remember Lady Stanmore coming here at any time!"

"I should have thought that as his widow she'd have wanted to inspect his belongings," said Charlesworth. "However, I'd like to inspect them. You don't mind?"

"Inspect anything you like," replied Gilford. "I'll leave you to it. But I doubt if you'll find much. He was a close man, Stanmore, when he liked, and he'd a way of covering up his tracks."

He went off and closed the door, and the detective, after a comprehensive look round the room, fell to examining the drawers in the writing-table and in a bureau that filled one of the recesses. But there was little to examine. Most of the drawers were empty or half-empty; none of them contained papers of a private nature. There was a cupboard in the room; one of its shelves held an array of wine and spirits; another a collection of cigar and cigarette boxes; here again nothing in the way of private papers was to be found. Eventually Charlesworth had nothing left to examine but an old desk of rosewood, clamped at its corners with brass, which he dragged out from beneath the bureau; in his opinion it had lain there untouched for a long time, for its lid was thick with dust.

The desk was locked, but to pick the lock and turn back the lid was child's play to Charlesworth. A scent of old and dried roseleaves rose to his nostrils as he found himself looking into this receptacle of a dead man's very private belongings, and to be sure there were roses in the upper tray of the desk, faded and crumpled but still possessed of some fragrance. There were the ghosts of other flowers, too, and a sprig here and there of lavender—Charlesworth began to realize that Stanmore, like most men, like himself, indeed, had a vein of sentiment in him. But he put his own aside and turned to his task. In the upper tray of this desk were two packets of letters, neatly tied and docketed. One proved to be letters written by Stanmore's father to Stanmore when he was at school; the other consisted of letters written to him by his mother. In that last packet was a lock of hair—dark, with silver threads running through it.

Charlesworth put these things carefully aside, and lifted the tray. It was scarcely out of his hands before he knew that he had hit on a discovery. There, staring him in the face was the photograph, old-fashioned, faded, of a pretty girl, unmistakably French, and with a name scribbled off in a bold, dashing handwriting in one corner—*Zélie*. And for one moment Charlesworth let his mind go back to his first inspection of Miss Irene Fawdale and his recollection of her face and features, and he knew that save for certain differences, hers was very like the face whose counterfeit he was looking at.

But there were other photographs—and all of the same subject. Evidently an actress, this Zélie—she was here in one costume; there in another; a comedienne, presumably. And suddenly amongst the photographs he found a folded play-bill of some seven-and-twenty years before, and scanning the names on it found that of Mlle. Zélie de Riancourt. Very well!—and what was Sir Charles Stanmore doing with all these things?

But now, beneath the dozen or so of photographs and the programme of the Théatre Victoire, Charlesworth found letters in the same bold, dashing script. It was one of his attainments to speak and read French with ease, and he sat down at Stanmore's writing-table and read letter after letter. Love-letters, of course, and varying in expression from the teasing and whimsical to the affectionate and tender. But when Charlesworth had gone through them and had become severely practical about the question of their value to him, he was face to face with certain facts:—

1st. Not one of the letters bore any address.

2nd. Not a single one carried any date.

3rd. It was impossible to make out the exact relationship of the writer to the person written to.

4th. There were no envelopes with the letters—and consequently no name and address of the addressee.

This was a serious *impasse*—but just as he was wondering how to get round or over it Charlesworth, beneath another, evidently later photograph, came across a letter in its envelope and knew that he had hit on yet one more link. For the letter bore a postmark and a date and the name and address of the addressee and on drawing out the sheet of letter-paper he found that there at last was a clue. For this letter was addressed to M. Charles Fawdale, 263, Greek Street, Soho, London, and it was dated from Mirranville-Sur-Seine, and it was signed Zélie, as all the other letters had been, and it informed its recipient that with prodigious and affrighting labours Zélie had now got the little but wholly adorable house in order, and that all that was now necessary was his, Charles', presence—together with certain other particulars entirely domestic and having chiefly to do with pots, pans, chairs, and tables.

Charlesworth made certain notes, put all the letters back in the desk, locked it up again, restored it to its hiding-place, and after a short interview with Gilford, went away. That night he crossed over to France, and so to Paris.

CHAPTER XVIII
THE SECOND VICTIM

Within twenty-four hours Charlesworth was in Paris, and on the evening of his arrival and with the aid of a map, he ascertained the exact whereabouts of Mirranville, which he made out to be a small place some fifteen miles outside the city, in the direction of Fontainebleau. By ten o'clock next morning he found himself in the one street of the village, wondering what connection so quiet and peaceful a spot could have to do with the business that had brought him there. For this was one of those French villages in which nothing seems to be going on. The men were at work in the fields, the women in the houses, the children in the school; there was scarcely a soul in sight as Charlesworth walked along the cobbled pavement. But he was quick to see that this was a place of charm; there was a winding river, and a many-arched and ancient bridge spanning it; there were picturesque old houses set amongst trees and gardens, and there was an old church, with the graves of many generations around its walls. Into that churchyard Charlesworth turned, after noting that almost opposite its gates stood an attractive hostelry, the Rayon D'Or. Before he had wandered five minutes amongst the cypresses he pulled himself up with a start—there, near the south transept of the church, in an evidently favoured position, stood a monument marked amongst the rest by a strange significance. From a marble-edged enclosure, carefully kept, and thickly planted with flowers of the season, rose a broken column which bore by way of inscription but one word, and that word a name—Zélie.

There was not much to go on in that, thought Charlesworth, but little as it was, it quickly led to results which he knew to be highly satisfactory. For in those quiet French villages time moves slowly and men live long, and within a few minutes of his discovery of the monument and its one word, Charlesworth was closeted with the venerable *curé* of the place who, as he was obviously delighted to observe, had exercised his ministry in Mirranville for half a century and to whom a mere twenty-five years span was as nothing. And M. le Curé remembered—everything. The broken column with the name Zélie?—ah, yes, monsieur must understand that it represented a story of the most pathetic! There had come to the village, some—yes, twenty-four-five perhaps twenty-six years ago, seeking a desirable residence, a beautiful and charming young woman, Madame Fawdale, who was accompanied by a maid—both French—Parisian. Madame found what she wanted—the little villa residence was still there for monsieur to see, if he desired—rented the desirable house and speedily furnished it from Paris. Then Monsieur Fawdale appeared on the scene—he was, monsieur would understand, an Englishman, handsome, rich, having, it was said, great interests in London; it was his habit to come to Mirranville every Friday and to return to London on Monday. He and Madame were devoted—ah, such lovers! And they were friendly, hospitable, charitable—the poor of Mirranville were very well aware of that, indeed! And so it lasted for nearly two years, and then—monsieur would comprehend—there was to be a baby. The baby came—but Madame went. There, under the broken column, she lies. The child—a girl, monsieur—the records of her birth and baptism, are they not in the books under the name Irene? What became of her? Monsieur entrusted her to the care of a good woman of the village—she still lives, that one, Mère Socart. In her care the child remained three years—Monsieur Fawdale came to visit her occasionally. Then, at the end of the three years, he took her away, placed money in his, the Curé's, hands for the perpetual care of the mother's grave, and went away. No, monsieur!—he has never returned.

Charlesworth, too, went away from Mirranville that afternoon, after interviewing Mère Socart and one or two other ancient inhabitants. And as he jolted back to Paris in the local train he arrived at three definite conclusions:—

1. That the young woman he knew as Irene Fawdale was undoubtedly the child of whom the Curé of Mirranville had told him.
2. That Sir Charles Stanmore, known to the Curé as M. Fawdale, was certainly her father.
3. That for some reason only known to himself, Sir Charles Stanmore had kept this passage in his life secret, and that Irene Fawdale had not the slightest knowledge of the true facts of her parentage.

That night, in his hotel in Paris, Charlesworth tried to get at an idea of where he stood in relation to the mystery of Sir Charles Stanmore's death. Whom did he really suspect? Upon whom was he going to attempt to fasten the crime? He had got to a stage where it was necessary to be definite. And eventually, chiefly influenced by his recently acquired knowledge of Irene Fawdale's undoubted selfishness and insistence on her own personal welfare, he came to the conclusion that it was she who had poisoned Sir Charles Stanmore, her motive being the desire to get him out of the way before he could alter his will—a course with which he had probably threatened her during the altercation between them overheard by Bedford. What actually took place during that altercation, and what was said, Charlesworth could only guess at, but he felt sure that in some way or other, Guy Stanmore came into it. And it was perhaps not an insignificant fact that he, Charlesworth, and Harding, on leaving the Manor on the morning after the discovery of the murder, should have seen the new baronet and Irene Fawdale in close conversation near the entrance lodge.

Well, there was still much to find out, and he must get back to England and set to work on it. He left Paris next morning by the 12.0 o'clock train, intending, as soon as reached London, to seek out Gilford at his private house and communicate to him the result of his investigations at Mirranville. But the purchase of an evening newspaper at Dover changed his intentions if not his thoughts. There, the first thing that caught his eye, he read, in bold black letters, spread across the top half of a page, an announcement that made him hasten to scan the succeeding columns:—

WEST END BOARDING-HOUSE MYSTERY

SUGGESTED RELATION TO THE ALDERSYKE MANOR CASE

POISONED CHOCOLATES

But if this startled Charlesworth and made him hurry to read, he was still more startled and made much more eager by catching sight of a name in the first few lines of leaded type. That name was *Purser*. Within a couple of seconds he knew what had happened to Purser and he saw daylight, too, as regards the Aldersyke Manor mystery.

This is what Charlesworth read; hurriedly at first, slowly and thoughtfully the second and third times:—

"The police authorities are busily investigating the circumstances attendant upon the death of a young woman named Margaret Purser, who was found early this morning dead in bed in her room at Number 611, Arbroath Street, Bayswater, a boarding-house of good standing kept by Mrs. Stradnell. There appears to be little doubt that the dead woman was the victim of a poisoner, and that the murder bears a close relation to the recent poisoning of Sir Charles Stanmore, at Aldersyke Manor, in whose service Margaret Purser had been for some years as parlour-maid. The police are by no means reticent in the matter, and we are able to give the following particulars from information supplied by them. It appears—from facts given by Mrs. Stradnell, proprietor of the boarding-house—that Margaret Purser took a room at 611, Arbroath Street, about three weeks or a month ago, which was shortly after the affair at Aldersyke Manor. Mrs. Stradnell's terms are fairly high, but Margaret Purser was evidently in a position to accept them, and from what Mrs. Stradnell saw of her she was in command of ample means. During the period of her residence under Mrs. Stradnell's roof she spent a great deal of money on clothing, and as she took Mrs. Stradnell into her confidence a good deal, Mrs. Stradnell knew that she paid ready cash for everything she bought. As to her way of spending her time, Mrs. Stradnell says that she attended a dancing class every afternoon and went to dances almost every evening, and she gathered from her that she was taking up dancing as a profession. Margaret Purser had also told Mrs. Stradnell that she had ample means of her own, and had recently come into a very handsome legacy.

"By the last post yesterday evening there was delivered at 611, Arbroath Street, addressed to Miss Margaret Purser, a package which is now, practically intact, in the hands of the police, and forms, of course, a most important clue. The package was taken from the postman by Mrs. Stradnell herself. She placed it on her parlour-table and handed it to Margaret Purser when the latter came in at eleven o'clock. Margaret Purser opened it there and then, in Mrs. Stradnell's presence. It proved to contain a pound-weight box of a certain well-known maker's mixed chocolates. On the top layer was an envelope from which Margaret Purser drew a sheet of letter-paper. She glanced over it, made a jesting remark to Mrs. Stradnell about its being a love-letter, and offered Mrs. Stradnell the chocolates. Mrs. Stradnell took two out of the box, and placed them on her mantelpiece saying that she would eat them next day. Margaret Purser gathered up the box and its wrappings and the letter, said good night and went to her room. Nothing more was seen or heard of her that night. At eight o'clock this morning, one of Mrs. Stradnell's two maids, Elizabeth Brown, took into Margaret Purser's room a cup of tea and some hot water. She found Margaret Purser dead in bed. According to the medical evidence she had been dead some hours. On a table by the bedside was the box of chocolates, of which the unfortunate young woman had eaten several before going to sleep. There has already been made some test of the chocolates in the box thus received and there is no doubt that many contain poison. As we have already stated, the police are in possession of the box, its wrappings, and the accompanying letter. The box itself bears the imprint of a famous maker of fancy chocolates, but there is nothing to show where it was retailed. The wrapping was an ordinary piece of brown paper on which there is nothing to betray its source. The address is typed on a gummed label. The accompanying letter is also typed. It is, as Margaret Purser remarked jokingly to Mrs. Stradnell, a love-letter of a rather silly sort. Obviously, the murderer sent it as a blind, thinking that Margaret Purser would believe it and the chocolates to have come from some anonymous admirer. The present theory of the police is that Margaret Purser, who was in service at Aldersyke Manor at the time of Sir Charles Stanmore's death, was in possession of some knowledge about his murderer which would have been fatal to the latter if divulged; that she was possibly blackmailing the murderer of Sir Charles, and that she has paid for her knowledge with her life. The question now to be answered is—who sent Margaret Purser the poisoned chocolates? And we may add to that the remark that whoever murdered Margaret Purser is presumably the murderer of Sir Charles Stanmore and a peculiarly cruel and callous danger to society."

Charlesworth paid little attention to the last words of this account—it went for granted that the murderer was all that this reporter said, and much more—the pertinent question was—who was the murderer? And again and again he harked back to Irene Fawdale. She was just the sort, he felt assured, to get rid of Purser in cold blood, doing the thing in calm, calculating fashion—as he believed she had done. Who was going to trace the sale of a box of chocolates of a well-known make? Thousands of such boxes were sold in London every day. Who was going to trace the identity of the sender of a typed letter and a typed address label? No—it had all been done very cleverly and with design to avoid discovery. Still—it would be something if the experts could prove that the poison used in the chocolates was akin to that taken from the Borgia Cabinet. What rather puzzled Charlesworth, however, was the murderer's present possession of poison presumably taken from the cabinet, which, he knew, had been taken away by the two doctors after their experiment on the old dog; as regards that, he could only surmise that the poisoner had possessed himself (or herself) of the particular poison used in sufficient quantity to destroy more victims than one.

The train sped on to London with its usual swiftness, but Charlesworth chafed impatiently until it reached Victoria, and he could hurry to Headquarters. There he met Sherman, a man with whom he had often worked, and whom he now found to be in charge of the Purser affair.

"Nothing beyond what you've already read in that," said Sherman, pointing to the paper in Charlesworth's hand. "Nothing!"

"Any further report about this particular poison?" asked Charlesworth.

"Only that the medicos seem to be certain that it's the same stuff that was used on Stanmore," replied Sherman. "Of course, this job's been done by whoever it was that did that! Purser knew too much."

"Show me the letter that was sent with the chocolates," demanded Charlesworth.

Sherman produced the letter—some half-dozen lines of mawkish stuff typed on a square sheet of flimsy paper. Charlesworth got an idea.

"Come along with me to Aldersyke Manor," he said. "We can run down there under the hour. And bring this letter with you."

CHAPTER XIX
THE DESERTED HOUSE

Sherman was a man in whom Charlesworth had great confidence, and as they journeyed down to Aldersyke Manor he told him the result of his inquiries in France.

"What's the idea?" asked Sherman, after listening carefully.

"That this young woman, Irene Fawdale, who's evidently the sort that always consider self first and the rest not at all, and utterly ignorant of the fact that Stanmore was her father, got rid of him before he could alter his will," replied Charlesworth. "I'm going on the supposition that when he and she had that row in his study the morning before his death he told her of what he was going to do. Well, she stood to lose five-and-twenty thousand!"

Sherman considered matters awhile in silence.

"The thing is," he said at last, "the thing is—so it seems to me, anyway—why did Stanmore wish to alter his will? What had happened? What had this young woman done? From all you tell me, he'd been taking extraordinary care of her all her life, spending no end of money on her, and all that sort of thing, and so on. Why such a sudden and extraordinary change of attitude?"

"That," replied Charlesworth, "is just what we don't know."

"It ought to be found out," declared Sherman. "But there's another feature. According to your account, Miss Fawdale wasn't the only person who was to be practically disinherited—that is, relatively: £500 a year instead of that lump sum of £25,000 which would have brought her in at any rate £1,250 a year. And that person the nephew—the new baronet. What had he done? The alteration in the young woman's case is a trifle compared to the alteration in his! If this chap Sir Charles Stanmore was a millionaire, or something like it, and if, as you say, the original will——"

"—*The* will," interrupted Charlesworth. "It stands!—according to Gilford."

"Well—you know what I mean," continued Sherman. "Call it the original will. It gives pretty nearly everything to Guy Stanmore, as successor to the baronetcy, and everything, I suppose, would mean a capital that would bring in forty to fifty thousand a year. But in the will that Sir Charles talked of making, Guy's cut down to a miserable £500 a year, exactly the same as the young woman! Now—what had *he* done?"

"Goodness knows!" muttered Charlesworth. "And how's one to find out?"

"It'll have to be found out. But I've an idea. I think this young man and this young woman, Guy Stanmore and Irene Fawdale, had been up to something of which Sir Charles strongly disapproved, that he was angry with them beyond hope of forgiveness. But—what?" concluded Sherman. "What?"

"I don't suppose anybody could answer that question but themselves," replied Charlesworth. "And anyhow, the new will hadn't been made. Sir Guy comes into nearly everything, and Irene Fawdale gets her £25,000."

"There were pretty handsome legacies to servants, weren't there?" remarked Sherman. "Rather unusual ones, eh?"

"They were well remembered," said Charlesworth. "And they've got theirs, already, so Gilford tells me. He's sole executor, and he's made sharpish work about getting *the* will admitted to probate and paying out the smaller legacies. Wants to clear up and wash his hands of the whole thing, I fancy. Well!—I don't think we shall be able to pull down our cuffs just yet, Sherman!—there's a lot to do."

"What are we going to the Manor for, now?" asked Sherman.

"I'll tell you—it may be a brain-wave. You noticed that the paper on which the letter to Margaret Purser was typed was a flimsy sort of stuff, didn't you?" replied Charlesworth. "Foreign note-paper, in fact—I noticed the water-mark on it, at once: I don't know if you did. But did you notice something else? About a couple of inches had been neatly and carefully trimmed off the top of the sheet! That struck me immediately. What had been on the strip of paper so removed? Obvious!—the address of some Continental hotel!"

"Well?" asked Sherman laconically.

"Well, I happen to know—I got a lot of information from Bedford, the butler at the Manor, at one time or another—I happen to know, I say, that just, or not very long before Sir Charles Stanmore's death, he and all the ladies of his family had been in France for some little time, a month or so, I believe. And I don't know if you're aware of it, Sherman, but I am—it's a very usual practice of English ladies when they're staying in foreign hotels to annex the hotel's note-paper and envelopes and there's generally specimens of each in their trunks or their dressing-cases when they return home. They don't mean to steal it, not they!—but they pick up paper and envelopes from writing-desks in hotels and pop them into their own writing-cases or blotting-pads or they carry them up to their own rooms—see? Fact, I assure you, if a small and unimportant one!"

"Well?" repeated Sherman.

"Well, I just want to see if there's any foreign note-paper lying about in the ladies' rooms at Aldersyke Manor," replied Charlesworth, "and, if there is, if it corresponds with the paper that you've got in your pocket. And—if there is, I think I shall be getting a bit nearer to a solution of this problem—who sent the poisoned chocolates to Margaret Purser? Eh?"

"Good notion!" agreed Sherman. "We can get free access to the house, then?"

"The butler I spoke of, Bedford, will let me go anywhere and give us every assistance," declared Charlesworth. "Most amenable and useful chap, that! He's been of the greatest help to me, all through. Taken a real interest in the case. Oh, yes, Bedford'll let us examine the house from top to bottom, if we like."

But when the car drew up at the gates of Aldersyke Manor, the house, seen across the intervening grounds and lawns, looked dark and deserted; not a single window showed a gleam of light, though dusk had fallen an hour previously. Charlesworth got out and went to the door of the lodge; the driver of his car had already found that the entrance gates were padlocked.

"We want to go up to the house," said Charlesworth to the woman who came to the door. "To see Mr. Bedford—he's there, I suppose?"

"Mr. Bedford's gone, sir," replied the woman. "He left two or three days ago. He's gone for good. Everybody's gone. Mr. Gilford came down the day they all went. The house is locked up. Of course, I have the keys—the house has been left in charge of me and my daughter."

Charlesworth hesitated a moment. Then he stepped over the threshold.

"Let me come in a moment," he said. He followed the lodge-keeper into her lighted living-room. "You've seen me before," he continued. "Detective-Sergeant Charlesworth you know. Let me see—you're Mrs. Marchant, eh? Well, Mrs. Marchant, I want to go into the Manor—police business. You can let me in?"

"Oh, I can let you in, sir," replied Mrs. Marchant, producing a bunch of keys from a drawer. "Mr. Gilford gave me strict orders about who I was to admit and who not to admit, but of course as I know you and as it's police business——"

Charlesworth called Sherman and together they followed the lodge-keeper up the drive and to a side-door. Mrs. Marchant turned on the electric lights and was about to go away, but Charlesworth detained her.

"A moment, Mrs. Marchant! Do you know anything about the arrangements in this house?" he asked. "I mean, do you know which rooms were occupied by Sir Charles, and which by Lady Stanmore, and so on?"

"Oh, yes, I know all that, sir," replied the lodge-keeper. "I've worked in the house at times when they were short of maid-servants: I know all the rooms, sir."

"Well, just show me which were Miss Fawdale's rooms," said Charlesworth. "And then you can leave us to look round—we may be some time."

Mrs. Marchant led the two men up the big staircase, along one or two corridors, and finally threw open the door of a room and stood aside.

"Very nice suite of rooms this is, gentlemen," she said, as if she had been the proprietor of an hotel showing his accommodation to possible guests. "Faces the south garden. You'll lock up all safe and bring me back the keys, sir?" she went on, turning to Charlesworth. "Of course, Mr. Gilford considers me responsible."

Charlesworth reassured her and when she had gone turned to his companion with a smile and a comprehensive wave of the hand.

"I dare bet any man a hundred pounds to a penny that in five minutes I find just what I expect to find in this room!" he said. "And to show how certain I am we'll examine this first." He walked across to a handsomely-appointed desk which stood between the windows and on which lay a litter of various things, books, magazines, papers, stationery. "Miss Fawdale doesn't appear to have carried away all her belongings, Sherman—in fact, this room looks as if she'd full anticipations of returning to it, and perhaps she had. Well, now, amidst all this paraphernalia, here's a lady's despatch case—just the sort of thing she'd carry on a journey. Let's open it, to start with. Now, then—there you are! What did I tell you?"

Sherman, glancing into the case which Charlesworth had snapped open, saw, lying loose amongst other matters, some sheets of foreign-looking note-paper and some envelopes. Instinctively his hand went to the pocket in which he carried the typed letter to Margaret Purser.

"Aye, get that out, and let's compare the papers!" said Charlesworth, drawing a sheet from the case. "Just what I said—hotel note-paper. See—Grand Hotel, Le Puy-en-Velay. Now look at your sheet—with the top cut off. Compare the paper. Same paper, Sherman. Same water-mark, Sherman! The only difference in the two pieces of paper is that from yours the French address has been neatly trimmed off with a sharp knife."

"Or scissors," suggested Sherman.

"No—a knife," said Charlesworth. "Scissors, even in the hands of a woman, wouldn't have cut such a dead straight line as that. Your sheet, Sherman, has been folded over, pressed down, then cut with a sharp-edged knife. Just an inch and a half trimmed off at the top, see. Now I wonder. . . ."

He suddenly paused, looked narrowly about him, and turned to drag out from where it was half concealed by a window-curtain a waste-paper basket, half-filled with litter. Amongst this he began to search, and presently sat down on the floor, the basket between his legs, systematically examining and going through every scrap of paper before him. Suddenly he looked up.

"Got it!" he exclaimed. "Look there, Sherman! That's the scrap that was cut off the top! It's been cut off in this room! Man!—the scent's getting hot!"

Sherman quietly pointed towards a recess close by.

"The letter may have been typed in this room," he observed. "There's a machine."

Charlesworth turned eagerly: he had another idea. Without a word he hastened across to the typewriter, took off its cover, and snatching up a sheet of the foreign letter-paper typed a few lines.

"Here, let's compare this lettering with the letter you've got there!" he exclaimed. "See? Identical! Sherman!—you may bet your last halfpenny that Purser letter has been typed in this room. And who's likely to have typed it but Irene Fawdale? Come on!—let's get out."

"Nothing else to inspect?" asked Sherman, phlegmatically. "While we're here——"

"No, come on!" replied Charlesworth. "I want to see that old woman again."

He hurried his companion out of the room and the house, turning off the lights as he went, and having locked the side-door by which Mrs. Marchant had admitted them, strode off towards the lodge.

"There you are, Mrs. Marchant," he said, placing the keys on the table. "We haven't been long, you see: nothing much that we wanted. So Mr. Bedford's gone, has he? And when was that?"

The lodge-keeper considered this question.

"Well, let me see, sir," she answered. "This is Friday, isn't it? Just so—well, it would be Tuesday when Mr. Bedford left. That day Mr. Gilford came down, and everybody left. Mr. Bedford, he told me he was going to see his relations, away in the North of England. He'd gone before Mr. Gilford came, sir. Mr. Gilford, he paid off the rest of the servants and handed the keys to me. He said, sir, that he didn't know what the new baronet, Sir Guy as now is, was going to do about taking up residence here and the house might as well be closed as have a lot o' servants in it, doing nothing and eating their heads off."

"And I suppose nobody's been since Mr. Gilford closed it and gave you the keys?" suggested Charlesworth. "That is till I came, just now?"

"Oh, yes, sir, somebody's been," replied Mrs. Marchant. "The day after they all left, Mrs. John Stanmore and Miss Fawdale came, in a car, sir. They said they wanted some things of theirs, and were surprised to find the house closed. Of course, I let them in, and they were there some time—I made 'em some tea while they was there—and took away two or three trunks with 'em in the car, sir. But otherwise, there's been nobody till you came, sir."

"Well, be particular about letting anybody in," said Charlesworth. "Stick to Mr. Gilford's orders. Of course, if we come again that'll be all right, Mrs. Marchant."

He hurried Sherman out then, and into the waiting car, and bade the driver get back to town and to Headquarters as quickly as possible.

"I've precious little doubt, now, Sherman," he said as they drove off. "Irene Fawdale is the woman we want! And to get her is the next move."

But when they reached Headquarters there was a new development. One of their fellow officials met them and beckoned them towards a waiting-room.

"There's a man here waiting for you, Charlesworth," he said. "He says he's Sir Guy Stanmore's orderly, a soldier, from Aldershot, and he's something to tell you."

CHAPTER XX
STRANGE REVELATIONS

Charlesworth, followed by Sherman, walked into the waiting-room, to find there a tall, well set-up young fellow in mufti, who, in spite of his straight glance and soldierly bearing was obviously shy, nervous, and uncomfortable. He stood up as the two detectives entered, looking inquiringly from one to the other.

"You want to see me?" asked Charlesworth encouragingly.

"Detective-Sergeant Charlesworth, sir?" inquired the visitor. "I do, sir!—saw your name in the papers about that Aldersyke Manor affair, so I asked for you. My name's Crabbett—John Crabbett. Private in the South Wessex Light Infantry. Orderly to Sir Guy Stanmore, sir."

Charlesworth pricked up his ears. What was coming? He turned to Sherman.

"Ask Inspector Colindale to come here," he said in an undertone. "Something to tell, Crabbett?" he asked as Sherman left the room. "Something about the Aldersyke Manor affair?"

"Not exactly about that, sir," replied Crabbett. "It's about—about the death of Miss Purser."

"Ah!" exclaimed Charlesworth. "You know something, eh?"

"It's more of what I'm—sort of uneasy about than what I know, sir. There's something strange that isn't mentioned in any of the papers I've read. So I thought well to come here—got leave to do so."

"Quite right," said Charlesworth. "Wait a moment, till Inspector Colindale comes. And bear in mind—you can say anything you like here, Crabbett! All between ourselves—at present. Don't be afraid of telling—anything."

Crabbett nodded and looked about him, silently, until Sherman came back with Colindale, a quiet, reserved man who listened to Charlesworth's explanation of Crabbett's presence before he spoke.

"You want to make a statement?" he said, turning to Crabbett. "Do you wish to have it taken down in writing?"

Crabbett looked puzzled.

"I don't know about a statement," he answered. "I came to tell what I know, and to hear what you've got to say about it. That was my idea, sir."

"Better let him talk," suggested Charlesworth. "We can have a formal statement later, if necessary."

Colindale sat down at a desk, folded his hands on its ledge, and nodded at Crabbett.

"Yes?" he said. "What do you want to tell?"

Crabbett was evidently at a loss as to how to begin. But he suddenly plunged into the middle of things.

"I think there's been foul play in this matter of Miss Purser!" he exclaimed. "Seems to me she was put away—wilful!"

"Murdered, you mean?" suggested Charlesworth.

"Looks like it," agreed Crabbett, angrily, "and if I can find out, definite, who it was——"

"Look here, Crabbett," interrupted Charlesworth. "Let's be precise. Had you some interest in Margaret Purser? Sweetheart, eh? Engaged, perhaps?"

"Well, not what you'd call definite, but as good," admitted Crabbett. "I'd seen a good deal of her since she came to London—used to come up and see her whenever I could get leave. You might say it was an understood thing."

"Well, why do you think there has been foul play? There has been foul play, of course!—it's an established fact that Purser was killed by eating poisoned chocolates sent by some person at present unknown. But what makes you suspect foul play?—what, particularly?"

Crabbett looked stolidly from one man to the other before speaking. Then he put a question.

"It's all on the strict confidential, this?" he asked. "All private? Well, in that case—I think Miss Purser knew something!"

"What about?" asked Charlesworth.

"That Aldersyke Manor affair!"

"You mean the death—murder, perhaps—of Sir Charles Stanmore?"

"Just that, sir!"

"Did she ever tell you that she did?"

"No! But—I made a pretty good guess at it."

"From what?"

"Well, there were things. Hints, like. Words, dropped now and then."

"Any names mentioned?"

"No! No names. She knew how to hold her tongue, did Peggie, when necessary!"

"Good hand at keeping secrets, eh?"

"She'd kept one very well," replied Crabbett, with a knowing smile.

"What was that?"

Crabbett hesitated a moment. Then he smiled again.

"Well, I reckon it's all got to come out," he said. "It was about the marriage of Lieutenant Stanmore—Sir Guy as now is."

"Marriage?" exclaimed Charlesworth. "Who's he married to?"

Crabbett went on smiling: the smile of a somewhat naïve personality that enjoys the possession of knowledge not shared by others.

"Well, it's to that Miss Fawdale—Lady Guy Stanmore as now is," he answered. "She knew that, did Peggie! And so did I!"

"Good Heavens!" muttered Charlesworth. Guy Stanmore married to Irene Fawdale! Whatever did that mean—and whatever complications were to arise from it? He stared at his two fellow officers and stared at Crabbett. And Crabbett smiled and nodded.

"Married a fair bit, them two," he remarked. "Peggie Purser and me, we knew. We were witnesses. That was when I first met Peggie Purser—never saw her before that day."

Charlesworth was recovering from his first surprise, and now he wanted to know everything that this evidently well-informed witness could tell.

"What do you mean by a fair bit, Crabbett?" he asked. "When were Lieutenant Stanmore and Miss Fawdale married?"

"It'll be about three months since," replied Crabbett. "At about that."

"And where were they married? You know that, of course."

"Of course—I was there. It was at Crondall Church, near Aldershot—Lieutenant Stanmore had taken rooms there so as to get a licence. One morning pretty early it was. We went over from Aldershot, him and me; Miss Fawdale and Peggie Purser came over from Aldersyke and met us there. Never saw Peggie before that day. Her and me, we spent that day together."

"After the wedding?"

"Yes, after that, of course. As soon as they'd got married, Lieutenant Stanmore and Miss F., Mrs. Guy then, she was, to be sure, went off in his car somewhere, to have their lunch; me and Peggie Purser were to look after ourselves till they came back in the afternoon. Of course, we were sworn to keep it all secret. And as far as I know, a secret it has been, where we were concerned. I never let it out to anybody, and I don't think Peggie ever did."

"Did Purser ever mention it to you, Crabbett, after Sir Charles

Stanmore's death?"

"I mentioned it to her. I asked her when they were going to make it known, and she said she reckoned they'd do so when all the affairs were wound up."

"You don't think she ever told it to anybody?"

"I don't think she did. Never heard of it, anyhow."

Charlesworth reflected for a moment or two. His mind went back to the evening of Sir Charles Stanmore's death.

"Can you remember anything, Crabbett, about Sir Charles Stanmore's affairs?" he asked. "Do you remember, for instance, anything that happened to Lieutenant Stanmore the day before he learned of his uncle's death?"

"Yes," replied Crabbett, readily. "I do! I remember that about noon that day he got a wire from Mrs. Guy. I saw it—he used to leave wires lying about. It asked him to go over that night as she must see him, at the usual time and place."

"What did she mean by the usual time and place?" asked Charlesworth.

"Why," replied Crabbett, grinning, "he'd been in the habit of running over there late at night and meeting her in the grounds—I'd been with him, driving the car, many a time!"

"I see! And did he go that night—in answer to the wire? He did?—and did you go with him? Very well—just try to recollect. Do you remember anything happening while you were waiting with the car outside the gates of Aldersyke Manor?"

"Yes!" replied Crabbett, promptly. "A man came out and walked sharply towards the village."

That, of course, was Mappleson, said Charlesworth to himself. He returned to his questioning.

"Well, do you remember anything about next morning?"

"Yes! A wire came to tell the Lieutenant that his uncle had been found dead in bed."

"How did he take it?"

"Seemed to bowl him clean out! Not—not grieving, you'll understand. Just as if—well, as if he couldn't make things out. Knocked him fair off his pins!"

"What did he do?"

"Got into the car after a bit—and after he'd got leave—and went off by himself."

"To Aldersyke?"

"S'pose so. He was away all day."

"I suppose you were on pretty confidential terms with Lieutenant

Stanmore, Crabbett, seeing that he employed your services as witness to his marriage," remarked Colindale, who had hitherto left the questioning of the orderly to Charlesworth. "Now did he ever say anything to you about his uncle's death?"

"No, sir—beyond saying, that morning he heard of it, that it was a damned sudden job!"

"Did he never talk to you about it—and matters resulting from it?"

"No, sir, except that he once remarked that now that he'd come into the title, it was just possible he'd resign his commission."

"What's he been doing since his uncle's death?"

"Going along in pretty much the same way, sir. I can't recollect any great difference. Once or twice Mr. Bedford, the butler at Aldersyke Manor, has been over to see him at Aldershot, but otherwise——"

Charlesworth pricked up his ears at that.

"What did Bedford want with Sir Guy?" he asked sharply.

"Can't say, sir. Business about the house, I suppose."

"Has Sir Guy ever gone over to Aldersyke lately?" continued Charlesworth.

"Once, sir. He went over there one afternoon a few days ago. Mrs. Stanmore, Sir Guy's mother, and Lady Stanmore—Miss Fawdale as was—went there."

Charlesworth wondered why the lodge-keeper had omitted to mention this fact to him and Sherman. But he turned to more practical topics.

"Where's Sir Guy now?" he asked.

"Can't say, sir. This morning he got a wire soon after breakfast, and he went off and got leave, for how long I don't know, and then went away in his car, without saying much to me about it, except that I should hear from him as to when he was coming back."

"You don't know where he went?"

"No, sir—don't know at all. He said nothing to me.

"What made you decide to come here?"

"Well, sir, I'd been reading all there was in the papers about Peggie Purser, and considering what I knew about private affairs, I began to get uneasy. So I got to see our Adjutant and told him in confidence all that I've been telling you. And I got twenty-four hours leave to come up here—to see you gentlemen. The Adjutant, he said—tell 'em everything!"

"And—you have, eh?"

"Can't think of anything else, sir."

"Let's see if I can help you, Crabbett. Now, have you ever seen Sir Guy and his wife together since Sir Charles Stanmore's death?"

"Only that time at Aldersyke Manor, the other day, sir."

"But do you know if they've been together anywhere—lived together?"

"I know this, sir. Every Saturday of late Sir Guy's gone to town until Monday morning. Usually, he went in the car, alone, but one week-end, when he didn't take the car, he 'phoned me on the Sunday evening, to take the car over early next morning, to an address he gave—Roxburgh Mansions. I did that, and when I got there I noticed on the board inside the hall Miss Fawdale's name, so I guessed that was where she lived in town, sir."

Charlesworth made a note of the address just mentioned and then put a final question to Crabbett.

"You really think, Crabbett, that Purser was in possession of some secret?"

"I do, sir! From things she let drop—hinted at."

"Such as—what?"

"Well, that she'd never want for money. Somebody found her in money—plenty! My belief, sir, is that she knew something about Somebody. And if you want to know what really brought me here, gentlemen, what I'm convinced of is that that Somebody, whoever it is, has done the poor girl in! Cold-blooded murder, that's what it is—and I hope you'll see justice done on the murderer! Wish to God I'd my hands on him—or her!"

CHAPTER XXI
ROXBURGH MANSIONS

Him . . . or her! When Crabbett had gone, with one more hearty curse on the murderer of his sweetheart, Charlesworth turned to Sherman with an expressive glance.

"I don't think—considering all we know—that there's much wrong with my theory," he said. "Seems to be getting strengthened at every turn!"

"What is your theory?—and what do you know?" asked Colindale. "Let me know."

Charlesworth told him, briefly, the full story of his recent inquiries and of what he and Sherman had discovered at Aldersyke Manor that evening.

"And my theory amounts to this," he concluded. "There seems to be no doubt that a day or two before his death Sir Charles Stanmore discovered something which roused his anger and set him so much against his nephew Guy Stanmore and against Irene Fawdale that he determined to alter his will and instead of leaving them a big lot of money to cut them down to a bare subsistence—£500 a year each. What that something was I've never been able to make out until now! But Crabbett's told us. It was the secret marriage of these two! How he discovered it, we don't know. But discover it he certainly did. Hence his row with Irene Fawdale, of which I heard from Bedford. Probably during that row he told her he was going to alter his will, and how. Well, she's a self-seeking young woman, from all I've learnt of her, and she was faced with—what? She'd married this young Guy, expecting that he'd not only come into the baronetcy, but into an enormous fortune as well——"

"She'd have had to wait for all that, though," remarked Colindale. "Sir Charles was only a middle-aged man, I believe?"

"Sir Charles was liable to die any minute," replied Charlesworth. "He'd something wrong with his heart, and Irene Fawdale was probably aware of it. Anyway, there was the fact. She and Guy were to be practically disinherited. Well, I figure it that she wasn't taking any chances. From all I've learnt about her she's cool, calculating, determined—not the sort to let anybody stand in her way, and we've got to remember that she hadn't the slightest idea that Sir Charles Stanmore was her father! Also she knew that because of evidently well-known domestic difficulties, Lady Stanmore would be much more likely to be suspected than anybody else. She knew, too—though, to be sure, everybody in the house did, apparently—all about the poisons in the Borgia Cabinet. And, in short, my theory is that in order to make sure of the money left to her and Guy Stanmore in the original will, a copy of which she had no doubt seen many a time, for there was one actually knocking around in Sir Charles' study, she poisoned Sir Charles the very night on which they'd had their row and before he could sign the new will which he'd told her he was going to make. I say that Irene Fawdale's the woman we want!"

"Purser?" suggested Colindale.

"All of a piece!" exclaimed Charlesworth. "It all fits in. Purser, without doubt, knew something, or fixed on something, or discovered something that convinced her that Irene Fawdale was the poisoner. It may be that she actually knew it, without doubt. Well, she blackmails Irene! She comes to London and enjoys herself on the money with which Irene supplies her, little knowing with what a cool, calculating woman she's dealing. Eventually, Irene sends her the box of poisoned chocolates. Lord!—what's plainer? The paper on which the letter accompanying the chocolates is typed is absolutely identical with paper found by me and Sherman there in Irene's room at Aldersyke Manor this afternoon; the typewriter used is identical with one also in that room: she was in that room, professing to have gone there to get some stuff of hers only a few days ago. Talk about circumstantial evidence. . . ."

"Sir Guy?" broke in Colindale.

"You mean—do I think him an accessory? No!" replied Charlesworth. "I should say he knew nothing about it—knows nothing about it now! She's the mainspring of all this—and we ought to lay hands on her at once!"

"Where's that place Crabbett spoke of—Roxburgh Mansions?" asked Colindale. "The name isn't familiar to me."

"I know," said Sherman. "Block of new flats in the Museum district—where they pulled a lot of property down a year or two ago. Good class."

"Well," remarked Colindale, after glancing at his watch, "it's pretty late, but how would it be if you both go round there, and see if you can hear anything—and perhaps see something of this young lady?"

"I am going—if it's midnight!" declared Charlesworth. "Sherman will come along with me. And if I get hold of her. . . ."

He shook his head expressively and followed by Sherman, left the building and chartered the first taxi-cab he saw.

"I reckon we've as good as got her, Sherman," he remarked as they drove off. "In my opinion it's a clear case!"

"Well—yes," agreed Sherman. "As you put it, it seems so. But that soldier chap said, you remember, that Sir Guy hooked it from Aldershot this morning, in answer to a wire. Well, I should say that wire was from her—I should say, too, that she's hopped it, and that her husband's gone after her."

"Why should she hop it?" asked Charlesworth.

"Probably got a bit frightened after reading the Purser stuff in the papers, and decided to make herself scarce for a time," suggested Sherman. "After all, she's a woman, and however cool and calculating she may be, I reckon that being a woman, she's got nerves. Bet you a fiver she's off!—they generally hop it, all of a sudden, after doing something they oughtn't to do."

"Well, she'll be good to trace," said Charlesworth with grim determination. "Especially if we can ascertain beyond doubt that she does live, or has lived, at these flats. And it's a satisfaction to get a definite object to follow."

"Aye, well!" replied Sherman, cynically. "I reckon we shall have some surprises before we're done! They always come!—in my experience."

Charlesworth experienced a surprise within a moment of reaching Roxburgh Mansions. Arrived there, he and his companion walked into a handsome entrance hall, on one wall of which they at once saw a notice-board in black and gold, bearing the names of tenants. And there, staring them in the face, was the plain announcement—

Sir Guy and Lady Stanmore. 2nd Floor.

A hall-porter, obviously an old Army man, and in a smart livery, came forward eyeing the two detectives with something like knowingness.

"Yes, gentlemen?" he asked. "Wanting somebody?"

Charlesworth, after eyeing his questioner narrowly, drew him aside.

"Look here!" he said. "Between ourselves, we're police officers, inquiring into that Purser case—you know? Purser was at one time in the employ of the Stanmore family at Aldersyke, and I want to make one or two inquiries about her of Sir Guy Stanmore. Do you know if Sir Guy's at home?"

"He isn't," replied the porter, definitely. "He's away, somewhere. He came here in his car this morning, from Aldershot, where he's stationed with his regiment, you know, and he and Lady Stanmore went off together an hour later. I don't know where they've gone—they took a bit of luggage with them, but not much."

"Oh?" said Charlesworth. He was taken aback. "Well, some other time, then. I suppose Sir Guy is to be found here?"

"Only at week-ends," replied the porter. "You'll find him at Aldershot—Stanhope Lines—any day between Monday and Saturday."

Charlesworth nodded and was about to turn away.

"I suppose Sir Guy's only lived here since his marriage?" he said.

"He's only lived here since that, of course," answered the porter, in the tone and manner of one who knew all about it. "Lady Stanmore as now is, Miss Fawdale as was, she's lived here ever since these flats was built. Original tenant, she was. Of course, when her and Sir Guy got married recently, they painted her name out on the board there, and put the new one in."

"Oh, lived here some time, has she?" remarked Charlesworth. "Ah!—now did you ever know of Sir Charles Stanmore coming here to see her? Sir Guy's uncle?"

"Sir Charles? Lor' bless yer, yes!" replied the porter. "Used to come here frequent, he did. Queer business about his death, wasn't it?" he continued, looking inquiringly at his visitors. "And this Purser affair, too—d'ye think they're mixed up? Now, I've seen Purser, myself!"

"You have, eh?" said Charlesworth. "When?"

"Came here, two or three times, of late, to see Lady Stanmore—Miss Fawdale as was. Oh, yes—she was in here not so many days ago. One day last week it would be. Sharp young woman—poor thing! Getting any further about clearing it up?"

Charlesworth made a non-committal reply and drew Sherman outside to the cab which they had kept waiting.

"So Purser used to visit Miss Fawdale as was, Lady Guy Stanmore as is, did she?" he remarked. "Um!—we keep hearing queer things! Now, how is it that Crabbett didn't know that? Anyway, if he did, he never mentioned it to us. But I'm sure he didn't. Strikes me, Sherman, that Purser was an underhand sort. Well—now I'm going round to see that Mrs. Stradnell, in whose house Purser died."

"It's nearly eleven o'clock," said Sherman, yawning.

"Don't care if it's twelve or thirteen o'clock," retorted Charlesworth. "Come on! Arbroath Street, Bayswater!"

There were lights in the windows of 611, Arbroath Street, late as the hour was, and Mrs. Stradnell herself, a somewhat faded, tired-looking woman, admitted them readily on hearing their business. But she sighed wearily when Charlesworth asked her for a little talk about her unfortunate boarder.

"I've told your people about all I know," she said as she ushered her visitors into her private sitting-room. "I've had a regular procession of them ever since the poor girl died. And those newspaper young men!—I'm sure they're worse than you police!"

"Aye, well, but you haven't had me to see you before, Mrs. Stradnell," said Charlesworth, assuming his most ingratiating manner. "And, you see, I've got a bit more light on this affair than anybody you've seen up to now—you'd scarcely believe it but I was engaged on this business this very morning in—where do you think? You'd never guess! Paris!—all that way off! So you see I'm sparing no pains. And I'm sure you're anxious to see justice done, eh?"

"It was a wicked crime, indeed!" responded Mrs. Stradnell. "Of course, I've no idea of who did it. The poor young woman evidently had some enemy, though you'd never have thought it. I found her inoffensive enough. A bit inclined to be gay and frivolous—but quite harmless."

"How long had she been under your roof?" inquired Charlesworth.

"Well, that would be the fourth week, when—when it happened," replied Mrs. Stradnell. "She came one Monday, and this last Monday was the fifth from that."

"Always paid you regularly, I suppose?" suggested Charlesworth.

"Every Saturday morning," assented Mrs. Stradnell. "Regular as clockwork. You see, she was of what I should call a confidential nature, and very friendly, and she sort of made a confidant of me, as regards certain things. Now every Saturday morning there came a registered letter for her—I've seen her open that letter more than once, and I know what it always contained. Two five-pound notes! One of these five-pound notes she always handed to me for her week's bill—I used to give her the difference in smaller change. I've the last five pound she gave me in my purse at this moment."

"You have?" exclaimed Charlesworth, eagerly. "Let me see it!"

Mrs. Stradnell produced the note at once. But Charlesworth, who had hoped that it might have the stamp of some local bank on it, was disappointed. It was a crisp new note, with nothing whatever on it. Still, he made a note of the number. "She never told you from whom she got this weekly payment?" he asked.

"She did not," replied Mrs. Stradnell. "She kept that to herself. Once, I remember, I remarked to her that she was a lucky young woman to have such a nice, regular income, and she replied that she could have more than that if she liked—it was only what she considered necessary for a week's outlay."

"Gave you the idea that there was a sort of unlimited fund at her disposal, eh?" asked Charlesworth.

"Well, I don't know about unlimited, but I certainly gathered from her that she could have more than ten pounds a week if she wanted it," said Mrs. Stradnell. "Of course, her bill with me was never more than three pounds fifteen, at the outside."

"What did she do with the rest of her ten pounds?" inquired Sherman.

"Oh, she spent a good deal on pleasure—going out," replied Mrs. Stradnell. "She was very fond of dancing—she meant to go in for it professionally, in the end. And she was fond, too, of finery—I can assure you she soon spent what was left of her ten pounds after paying me! She wasn't extravagant, but she spent freely. I remember that the last Saturday she paid me, she laughed as she drew the two five-pound notes out of the registered letter and said it was a good job it had turned up punctually, for she was dead broke! Yes, only last Saturday morning that was!" concluded Mrs. Stradnell with a sigh. "There's the registered envelope her money came in—she threw it aside when she'd taken the notes out of it, and somebody put it on the mantelpiece there."

Before the words were well out of Mrs. Stradnell's mouth, Charlesworth had possessed himself of the thing she indicated—half-hidden behind an ornament. Without a word he drew something out of the envelope and in similar silence showed it to Sherman—a blank sheet of the same foreign note-paper that they had found that afternoon in Irene Fawdale's room at Aldersyke Manor.

CHAPTER XXII
WASTE PAPER

Charlesworth drew Sherman aside and pointed significantly to the blank sheet of paper which he had withdrawn from the registered envelope, and then to the postmark on the envelope itself.

"Look here!" he whispered. "See this?—and that? This paper is precisely similar to that foreign stuff we found at Aldersyke! And look at this postmark. This letter, enclosing the five-pound notes of which Mrs. Stradnell told us, has been registered—do you see where?"

"West Central Office, New Oxford Street," replied Sherman, promptly. "Well, what of that?"

"About the nearest main office to Roxburgh Mansions—that's all," said Charlesworth. "It's a clue, anyhow—and I'm going to follow it up." He turned to Mrs. Stradnell. "What do you do with your waste paper, Mrs. Stradnell?" he asked. "I don't mean newspapers and so on, but this sort of thing—letters and papers that get thrown aside or torn up by your boarders in these rooms?"

"Well, it isn't wasted, in one way," replied Mrs. Stradnell. "The waste-paper baskets in the various rooms are emptied into a sack, and once a month the sack's called for."

"Good plan!" said Charlesworth, with a sigh of hopefulness. "Have you a sack or so now?—that hasn't been emptied lately? You have? Good! Can we see it?"

Mrs. Stradnell led her visitors to the basement, where, in a corner of the cellar, stood a large sack, bearing the name of a firm of waste-paper dealers, and evidently full to the brim.

"Looks as if it hadn't been emptied lately," remarked Charlesworth.

"They didn't call for it last month," said Mrs. Stradnell. "Sometimes they forget. So there's two month's waste in it."

"All the better for what I want," replied Charlesworth gaily. "I'll borrow this from you, Mrs. Stradnell. Give a hand, Sherman."

Between them the two men carried the sack upstairs and out to the taxi which they had kept waiting; the cabman viewed the sack with surprise.

"Ain't got no dead bodies nor portions thereof in there, have yer, guv'nor?" he asked half-seriously. "Can't be too partik'ler, ye know!"

"Take a feel at it, my lad," answered Charlesworth. "Important State papers—that's all. Going to be short rations of sleep for you and me to-night, Sherman," he went on, as the cab moved off on its way to his rooms. "I'm going right through this little lot, and you've got to give a hand."

"What's the idea?" asked Sherman, gloomily.

"To see if there are any more of those registered envelopes in this sack, and if so, where they were posted," replied Charlesworth. "That remittance, you see, that Mrs. Stradnell told us of, has evidently been sent to Purser regularly for the past three or four weeks, and was always in a registered packet. Now, if we can find the envelopes and ascertain the office of origin, we shall be getting pretty close to what I'm determined to find out. And that is—who sent Purser ten pounds every week-end? For that ten pounds, Sherman, was—hush money!"

"You've got one postmark," remarked Sherman. "And as you say, that office isn't far off Roxburgh Mansions. Of course, you suspect Lady Guy?"

"It's fastening itself on her, bit by bit, in my opinion," admitted Charlesworth. "She didn't know that Sir Charles was her own father! All she knew, and cared about, was that he was going to cut her and her husband down to a miserable five hundred a year each and that he'd got to be put out of the way, carefully, before he could do it. But—Purser must have known of it! Probably she saw something."

"How do you know Purser wasn't an accomplice?" suggested Sherman.

"Not before the fact, I think," said Charlesworth. "Afterwards—yes, in the sense that she knew. Plain as a pikestaff, in my opinion," he went on. "A clear case—I think!"

"Well, there's one thing I don't hear any mention of," remarked Sherman. "You don't mention it, and there's no particular talk of it at Headquarters. Where's that necklace?"

"Ah!" exclaimed Charlesworth. "If we knew that! But I should say the answer to that question's pretty evident. The guilty party's got it! Of course!"

"Murder—and robbery, then," said Sherman. "But if your theory's correct, not murder for the sake of robbery. Still, I should have thought that if Sir Charles had been removed just to prevent him from making that new will and destroying the first, whoever it was that removed him wouldn't have bothered about the necklace. That wouldn't alter matters!"

"The necklace was probably appropriated by the murderer in the hope that we should conclude that it was the cause of the murder," replied Charlesworth. "Of course, its disappearance, and a description of it has been made known everywhere, in every likely place where it could be disposed of—here, Paris, Amsterdam, New York, and so on, but nothing's been heard of it. In my opinion, it's safely put away—and by the same hand that sent these registered letters to Purser."

Sherman rubbed his chin, in silence. He appeared to be thinking.

"Didn't it come out that Sir Charles carried that necklace in his trousers pocket—or something of that sort?" he asked.

"Something like that," assented Charlesworth. "Careless about it, anyway. Why?"

"If he had it loose in a pocket when he went to bed that night, what was there to prevent anybody from pinching it when Sir Charles was found dead in bed?" asked Sherman. "Servants, for instance? There was a footman, if I remember rightly, and there was that butler chap—Bedford. Either of 'em could have gone through his pockets before raising the alarm."

"The footman struck me as quite an honest sort of chap," replied Charlesworth, "and as for Bedford, I should say he's the personification of propriety. No!—the necklace had gone before the footman drew the blinds and made his discovery. But here we are—and we'll get to work on this sack of scrapped paper."

Charlesworth lived in a bachelor flat, the living-room of which was of considerable size. First giving his companion a scratch supper, and then moving some of the furniture aside so as to leave a clear space in the middle of the floor, he shot out the upper half of the contents of the sack, divided that half into two piles and bade Sherman set to work on one while he gave his attention to the other. Sherman glanced ruefully at the clock, and groaned as he got on his knees to begin his task.

"Seem to have been particular to tear up their paper into the smallest possible bits!" he grumbled. "Nice job this, anyhow!"

"Got to be done if it takes all night and all to-morrow!" declared Charlesworth. "Look out for anything in the way of a registered envelope or fragments of it, and for pieces of that foreign note-paper."

It was then one o'clock in the morning; at half-past two Charlesworth had got what he considered sufficient evidence to warrant him in calling off further research. The results of his and

Sherman's grubbing amongst the waste lay on Charlesworth's desk, spread out on a clean sheet of blotting paper. He tabulated them in his note-book.

1. A registered envelope bearing postmark of an E.C. office.
2. A registered envelope bearing postmark of Aldershot.

And—most important of all——

3. Another, bearing postmark of *Aldersyke*.

Charlesworth put his pencil point on the last-named.

"That's significant!" he said. "Look at the date. It was just about then that Sir Charles was poisoned—and it's evidently the first of the registered letters sent to Purser. Aldersyke! Sherman, we must go down there first thing in the morning! But we'll have to see the postal authorities before going, and get the proper authorization to examine the books there."

Then he and Sherman bundled the waste paper back into its sack and went to bed . . . but Charlesworth lay awake for some time, thinking, and maturing his plans. He was resolved and ruthless by that time, and at the end of all his speculations saw Irene in the dock. Irene . . . the cool, the calculating . . . it could be nobody else. And . . . her own father!

By half-past eleven that morning, Charlesworth and Sherman, accompanied by a post-office official, were down at Aldersyke. The post-office official laughed as they approached the little post-office.

"About a five minutes job, this!" he remarked, looking round him at the evidence of scanty population. "I don't suppose they register half-a-dozen letters in a month, here."

"What's of importance to us is the quality of the post-mistress' memory," said Charlesworth. "Can she remember who it was that despatched a particular letter on a particular date?"

"If it's not too far back, I should say she can," replied the official. "Village folk generally have pretty good memories for little things of that sort. It depends on what sort of woman this is—all I know about her is that she's had charge of this office for some years."

The post-mistress turned out to be a shrewd, sharp-eyed woman who narrowly inspected the official's authorization before she allowed him to see her books. But when the book of duplicate receipts of registered letters was placed before him and his companions, his prophecy that it would not be a heavy job to find what Charlesworth wanted was justified. Charlesworth pointed to the entry at once.

"There you are!" he said. "Miss M. Purser, c/o Mrs. Stradnell, 611, Arbroath Street, Bayswater, W.2. And the date's four days after the death of Sir Charles Stanmore. Well, now, who sent off this letter? That's what I want to know."

The official fetched in the post-mistress, who, in spite of his assurances, was obviously disinclined to tell anything, and regarded Charlesworth and Sherman with looks of strong disfavour.

"We're not supposed to give any information about any post-office business," she said, demurringly. "It's against——"

"You know who I am, Mrs. Jones," interrupted the official. "I've shown you the authorization."

"Yes—to inspect that book, but not to tell anything else," retorted Mrs. Jones. "I don't know that I'm doing right——"

"I may as well tell you, then, that you are," said the official. "These gentlemen are detectives! They've got permission to see anything here and to ask you any questions. I'm here to see that they get whatever information they ask for, and you can throw all responsibility on me."

"Oh well, of course, if it's like that——" remarked Mrs. Jones. She looked at Charlesworth, a little less sourly. "What might you be wanting to know?" she inquired.

Charlesworth pointed to the entry about which he was concerned.

"There's a duplicate here of the receipt given to the sender of a registered letter addressed to Miss M. Purser," he said. "I want to know, Mrs. Jones, if you can remember who the sender was?"

Mrs. Jones gave a mere glance at her own writing.

"Oh, yes!" she answered. "We don't have so many registered letters here that I can't remember that bit! It was Mr. Bedford, the butler."

Charlesworth concealed his surprise—Bedford had been the last person he had dreamed of hearing of as the sender!

"You're sure of that?" he asked.

"Oh, quite sure, mister! Mr. Bedford, he sent off two registered letters that afternoon," replied Mrs. Jones. "Leastways, one was a letter, and the other was a packet. There's the receipt for the packet, next to that for the letter," concluded Mrs. Jones who, now that she had once spoken, seemed inclined to speak freely. "Of course, I recollect it well enough—it's not so long since."

Charlesworth looked at the second receipt. The address was Mrs. Macdowall, 331, Belvidere Street, Hampstead Road, London, N.W.1.

"A packet, eh?" he said, meditatively. "Um!—he sent off both these—the letter and the packet—at the same time?"

"Same time—same day," replied Mrs. Jones. She stood gazing at her visitors, and especially at Charlesworth, as if wondering what they really wanted. "Of course, I shouldn't like Mr. Bedford to know that I'd told anything about his private business!" she continued. "If he comes back here——"

"You can be quite easy, Mrs. Jones," answered Charlesworth. "Mr. Bedford won't hear anything of this."

He signified to the post-office official that he had got what he wanted, and they left Mrs. Jones' cottage.

"Satisfactory?" inquired the official.

"May be," replied Charlesworth. He was not going to say that he had just had a big surprise. "Highly useful, anyway, and——"

He broke off there—pulled up by the sudden appearance of Gilford, who came round the corner from the railway station. Charlesworth ran across the road to him.

"Lucky you should turn up just now!" he said. "I say!—do you know where Bedford, the butler, is to be found?"

Gilford gave him a queer look.

"No!" he answered. "But I can tell you something about him!"

CHAPTER XXIII
THEORY IN FULL

There was a curious significance in Gilford's tone which made Charlesworth start and eye him inquisitively. The solicitor, in his turn, glanced questioningly at Sherman.

"One of your men?" he asked.

"Exactly!—he knows all about things," replied Charlesworth. He edged nearer to Gilford's side. "Something new?" he inquired.

Gilford shook his head. There was that in the movement which suggested more than Charlesworth, at the moment, could understand.

"I don't know what to make of certain things—exactly," said Gilford. "I think there's something—underneath, you know—that we're utterly ignorant about. This man Bedford, now—he came to see me, the other day. Privately, you understand?—but I'm not going to keep it private from you police people, for I think you ought to know. Bedford, after some sparring about, wanted to know if the new baronet was coming into his uncle's property. And—I could see that he was uncommonly anxious to be informed on that point, and I wondered why!"

"Yes?" said Charlesworth.

"Of course, I asked him why he came there to put such a question—what concern was it of his? He hummed and hawed for awhile, but I got it out of him at last. And—it was what I expected! Bedford had been in the habit of lending Master Guy money!"

Charlesworth started again.

"Ah!" he exclaimed. "He had, had he? On Guy's expectations?"

"I suppose so—though, considering that Stanmore was of little more than middle-age, the expectations were not likely to be speedily realized, were they?" replied Gilford. "But anyway, there was the fact. Bedford had lent young Guy ready money from time to time, because, according to Guy, his mother and his uncle kept him on short allowance. And, in the end, it amounted to a tidy little sum. How much do you think?"

"No idea—can't even guess. Five hundred?"

"Five fiddlesticks! Bedford wants five thousand some hundred pounds from Sir Guy—say, six thousand pounds!"

"Exorbitant interest, I suppose?"

"No interest at all—that's to be agreed upon at settlement. That's the actual amount of solid cash lent. And—Bedford holds papers for it. Promissory notes—I.O.U.'s, and so on. There's no doubt about it. Bedford showed me his documents and a little book in which he'd kept the account."

"Well?" inquired Charlesworth, after a pause during which his mind worked at express speed.

"Well, Bedford wants his money. He wants to buy some hotel property. And he'd been to Aldershot, bothering Sir Guy about it. Guy referred him to me."

"Will he get his money?"

"Oh, he'll get it, in time. We're winding things up as quickly as we can. But. . . ."

Gilford paused, looking at Charlesworth as if to invite some remark.

"Yes," said Charlesworth, understanding this glance. "But I don't know what to say! What do you say?"

"I say that there were—as we're beginning to find out—some very queer things occurring about the time of Stanmore's death," replied Gilford. "This is another of them. What I'd like to know is—had Stanmore found out that Guy had been borrowing money from Bedford? Had that anything to do with his resolve to make a new will and cut Guy down to a miserable five hundred a year? Stanmore was evidently very angry with Guy about something or other——"

"Stop a bit!" interrupted Charlesworth. "I've something to tell you that I only heard of last night and that I'm sure you're not aware of. Do you know that Sir Guy Stanmore is married?"

It was Gilford's turn to start. He turned a stare of incredulous astonishment on the detective.

"Guy Stanmore—married!" he exclaimed. "Nonsense!"

"True enough," said Charlesworth. "He was secretly married some little time before Sir Charles' death. There's no doubt about it."

"But—to whom?" asked Gilford.

"You'd never guess! Irene Fawdale!"

The solicitor's stare of astonishment turned to one of utter perplexity.

"Impossible!" he said. "Irene Fawdale? Why—what about the charge Lady Stanmore brought against——"

"Look here, Mr. Gilford," interrupted Charlesworth, "I know more than you're aware of, and as a matter of fact I was going to see you, probably this afternoon, to tell you what I've discovered, and what I've been informed of. Listen!—I've solved the mystery about Irene Fawdale. Do you know who she is? You don't?—and what's more, she herself doesn't know! She's Sir Charles Stanmore's daughter!—her mother was a Frenchwoman, an actress, or dancer; she's dead, long since, and I've seen her grave. I've traced Irene from her birth right up to the time Sir Charles brought her away from school, and what I tell you is the truth—though she's not aware of it, she's his daughter. And Sir Guy and she are married—that's a fact!"

"How did you find out about the marriage?" asked Gilford. "And when?"

"Only last night. Sir Guy's orderly, a young fellow named Crabbett, came to Headquarters and told us. Crabbett witnessed the marriage, at a village church near Aldershot. And so did Purser."

"Purser! The woman who's been poisoned—as Stanmore was!"

"Exactly! Purser—who was poisoned as Stanmore was!"

Silence fell on the three men. Gilford and Charlesworth continued to stare at each other.

"What do you make of it?" asked Gilford at last.

"If you want the plain truth," replied Charlesworth, "I think that Sir Charles found out about this secret marriage, and that he was so furious about it that he determined to alter his will. I think Irene Fawdale or Stanmore, as she was by then, knew of his intention, and that she got rid of him before he could. And, from certain things I've just learnt, I think that it's highly probable that Bedford knew something about it, and that we may find he was an accessory."

"Why Bedford?" asked Gilford.

"I've just found that Bedford has sent registered letters, containing money, to Purser! Hush money, without a doubt. And," concluded Charlesworth, "I must find Bedford! You've no idea where he's to be found?"

"He told me he was moving about—looking out for a desirable hotel property," replied Gilford. "But now I come to think of it, he did say where a letter would find him in London. Care of a Mrs.—Mrs.—ah, I can't remember the name, nor the address, but my clerk has a note of it, I fancy——"

Charlesworth glanced at his note-book.

"Was it Mrs. Macdowall, Belvidere Street, Hampstead Road?" he asked.

"That was it!—I remember now," assented Gilford. He glanced at Charlesworth's car. "Are you proposing to go there?" he asked. "Now?"

"This moment!" declared Charlesworth. "I'm going to have things out with Bedford!"

"Give me a lift back to town, then," said Gilford. "I can leave my business at the Manor for a day or two; it's of no great importance. But I say, Charlesworth," he continued, as the car moved off towards London, "do you really mean all you say—about the new Lady Stanmore? A poisoner!—and of her own father? It's—almost unbelievable!"

"She doesn't know that Sir Charles Stanmore was her father," replied Charlesworth. "He kept all that carefully from her, and from everybody—so well, indeed, that I don't think anyone but myself knows, with the exception of those, like you, to whom I've told what I discovered by investigation. But in the course of that investigation I found out a good deal about Lady Stanmore's character. Everybody who's had anything to do with her lays stress on one remarkable characteristic of hers—her utter selfishness and determination to let nothing stand in her way. She was evidently like that from being a mere child—on that point all the people who brought her up are agreed. Now put it to yourself! She marries this young Guy, secretly—why, Heaven only knows, but probably because she knew, well enough, that Sir Charles, for reasons of his own, would never give his consent to such a marriage. Well, somehow or other—I've not the remotest idea how!—Sir Charles finds out that these two are married. He's furiously angry about it——"

"How do you know that?" interrupted Gilford.

"He had a row with Irene the last morning of his life," replied Charlesworth. "It would be about that, of course! And already he'd seen that solicitor who came to see you, you remember—seen him about altering his will. Of course he was angry—just the sort of man who'd be intensely angry with any member of his family who did anything serious before consulting him or getting his consent, and no doubt he threatened Irene with all sorts of pains and penalties. But what would chiefly affect her would be the threat to cut her and Guy down to £500 a year each!—when she'd been all her life used to having everything she wanted. Moreover, here's another point. Sir Charles wasn't dead, then, and both Guy and herself were entirely dependent on him. How do we know that when they had that row, Sir Charles didn't threaten her with a stoppage of all supplies? Where would Mr. and Mrs. Guy Stanmore have been?—they couldn't live on Guy's pay! But she knew that the old will was in existence, and what its provisions were, and that it would probably remain in existence for perhaps a few days, certainly for twenty-four hours.

She knew, too, that if Sir Charles died before that old will was destroyed and replaced by the new one she and Guy would be all right. And so—well, Sir Charles had just got to be quietly put out of the way. And . . . she lost no time about it! Look here!" continued Charlesworth, growing still more earnest in his arguments. "I've come to the conclusion that Sir Charles didn't keep what Dr. Serracold told him to himself—you remember that Serracold, after examining him, formed the opinion that his heart was so bad that he might go any time, and told him so? Well, I think Sir Charles let his family know that—he seems to me to have been just the sort of man who'd take a sort of malevolent delight in frightening people, and perhaps he himself didn't believe Serracold."

"I think he did, though!" exclaimed Gilford.

"Why do you think so?" asked Charlesworth.

"Because of his apparent haste to get that new will made," replied Gilford. "If he'd been certain of a longer life he wouldn't have been in any haste."

"Well, maybe," agreed Charlesworth. "But, anyway, I think Irene knew what Serracold had said. And she probably argued that if she got rid of Sir Charles by using some stuff out of the Borgia Cabinet, everybody, doctors included, would say he'd died of heart failure and nobody would be suspected of poisoning him. A very calculating young woman it is that I'm talking of, you know!"

Gilford shivered a little.

"Ugh!" he said. "It all seems so—so cold-blooded! And—her own father!"

"I tell you—for the third time—she didn't know Stanmore was her father: she'd been brought up in the notion that he was her guardian," retorted Charlesworth. "He'd never given her a chance of learning the truth—didn't want her to!"

"Even then—her guardian!—it's cold-blooded," said Gilford. "Hideously cold-blooded! Murder!—of the worst sort! And—a woman!"

"Well, and what of that?" asked Charlesworth, with a cynical laugh. "What about Messalina? And Lucrezia Borgia? Weren't they women? Strikes me, sir, that for cold-blooded, determined, ruthless murder the women can lick the men every time! And in this case the motive was—somewhere about a million of money. A million!—or near it . . . and the lady, I think, has somewhat extravagant tastes. Come, now!—do you think she was going to allow a little sentiment to stand between her and fifty thousand a year? I don't!"

Gilford shook his head.

"You're a cynical chap, Charlesworth!" he said. "Cynical!"

"No!" protested Charlesworth. "I'm just an ordinary common sense sort of chap—no more. And what I've said is common sense."

"But this Bedford?" suggested Gilford. "Where does he come in?"

"Ah!" exclaimed Charlesworth. "I'm beginning to think that Bedford is a very deep, sly, scheming fellow!—I daresay he's had me on toast more than once! Well, I think Bedford knows something! And if he does—by George, I'll have it out of him, one way or another. Let's hope we find him at this address."

Belvidere Street, duly reached, proved to be a drab, down-at-heel side street, in one of the poorer parts of the Hampstead Road. Charlesworth purposely stopped the car at the entrance.

"It won't do for us all to go down there," he remarked. "You go, Sherman—you have the number—and find out what you can. If Bedford's in, signal to me; if not, try to get an idea as to where he's to be found or when he's to be back. Keep your eyes and ears open."

Sherman went down the street; within a minute they saw him talking to a woman at an open door. Presently he came slowly back.

"He's not in," he announced. "The landlady says he said he was going to see some lawyer or other."

CHAPTER XXIV
IN STRICT PRIVACY

Charlesworth motioned Sherman to reenter the car, and turned to Gilford.

"That'll be you, Mr. Gilford!" he said. "He's after his money again. Let's go along to your office."

"I doubt if it's me that he's after," replied Gilford. "I told him plainly that I could do nothing for him until things were settled, and in any case until I'd seen Sir Guy. But you can come along there, if you like, on the chance."

There was no news of Bedford, however, when they reached the office, but there was news of another sort. One of the clerks stopped Gilford as he was taking the two detectives into his private room.

"Mr. Mappleson called to see you, sir," he said. "Half an hour ago, that was. As I couldn't tell him when you'd be in, he asked if you'd ring him up at the First Avenue Hotel as soon as you got here—he wants to see you on a matter of pressing importance and as soon as possible. Either that, or would you go round to see him—he'll be in there all the morning?"

Gilford looked at Charlesworth and saw that the detective had caught Mappleson's name and had pricked up his ears at the sound of it.

"We'll go round," he said. "It's only a stone's throw. Come on, both of you. Now," he continued when they had got outside the office, "what's all this about?—why does Mappleson want me and what's his business that it's of such pressing importance? Has it anything to do with this Stanmore affair?"

"If you're asking me," replied Charlesworth, "I should say—yes! What else? Mappleson, after all, knew things. Perhaps," he added, with a significant smile, "he now knows more."

Mappleson, found reading a newspaper in the lounge of the First Avenue, betrayed an evident relief at the sight of Gilford and Charlesworth, and after a hasty inquiry as to Sherman, led his three visitors into a quiet corner of the smoking-room. It was obvious that he had news, and was anxious to impart it.

"I'm very glad you've turned up," he said. "I was rather afraid from what they told me at your office, Mr. Gilford, that you might be out of town all day—in fact, I was just thinking of finding Charlesworth, but I didn't know, exactly, how to set about it. And something has come to my knowledge which, in my opinion—though, mind you, I may be wrong—in my opinion, I say, may have to do with the mystery of our late friend Charles Stanmore, and I wanted to acquaint you with what I know as speedily as possible. Now, look here—you remember everything about the Verringham necklace, and all that I told you?"

"Everything!" replied Charlesworth.

"You police people have never traced it?"

"Not a trace! Never been able to hear a whisper of it!"

"Well, now, I'll tell you something. You are aware that I am connected with the trade in precious stones, and especially in diamonds—international trade. Well, there came to me, privately, last night, knowing that I was in town, a man of whom I have some slight knowledge. His name is Ehrenfeldt, and he is a diamond merchant, in a not very big way of business, in Hatton Garden, close by here, you know. He is, I think, a decent and an honest man, but very unfortunately for himself, he was drawn, some few years ago, into a rather nasty case of alleged fraud, in connection with a transaction in diamonds, and though he was cleared, and it was proved that he had been a catspaw in the hands of unscrupulous scoundrels, it has made him very chary and suspicious of anything but absolutely above-board transactions."

"I remember the case you mention," remarked Charlesworth. "It was a Central Criminal Court case in which Ehrenfeldt and three other men were charged. Ehrenfeldt, as you say, was acquitted; the others got it pretty heavy."

"Well, Ehrenfeldt doesn't want to run any more risks," said Mappleson. "Which explains why he came to me, last night, with his story. And I may tell you that why he came to me was because he remembered my name in connection with the Verringham necklace. Now his story is this. He says that yesterday afternoon there came to him, in his office in Hatton Garden, a highly-respectable man who after some preliminary, general talk about selling valuables in the way of precious stones, told Ehrenfeldt that he was steward and major-domo to a North of England family which, by agricultural depression and the like, had been considerably reduced in circumstances and was under the necessity of realizing ready money on certain of its possessions. He went on to say that the present head of the family, a widow lady, possessed a quantity of loose diamonds, which she was anxious to sell for cash; she was also anxious that the transaction should be an absolutely private and confidential one, as she didn't want the affair to get known to friends or the public. In short, was Mr. Ehrenfeldt prepared to buy? Of course, Ehrenfeldt wanted to know how his visitor chanced to come to him? The man replied that it was by mere chance that he came—he knew that the diamond trade is centred in Hatton Garden, so he had come there, looked about him, and had called on Ehrenfeldt as he might have called on any one of his neighbours. Next Ehrenfeldt asked where and when the diamonds could be seen? His visitor replied that he had been entrusted with a few of them, and he produced these from his purse. Now Ehrenfeldt is a practical man, and of considerable experience, and he saw at once that these stones were, first, of great value, and second, that they had been detached from a necklace!"

"Ah!" exclaimed Gilford. "From a necklace!"

"Undoubtedly—he said. Well, Ehrenfeldt, like everybody else, I suppose, had read about the disappearance of the Verringham necklace—anyway, he immediately thought of it. But, of course, he said nothing of that to his visitor. What he did was to put two or three questions of a fishing nature to him—to find out if the man had any idea of the value of the diamonds. He came to the conclusion that he had a very good idea! Then, he wanted to know who it was that he was asked to deal with? The visitor replied that the lady desired to preserve her anonymity. That, replied Ehrenfeldt, would never do—he, in his own interest, must know the name of the vendor; must, indeed, know her; must be satisfied of her *bona fides*. And eventually, he and his visitor arranged that the latter should bring his principal, the widow lady, to Ehrenfeldt's office at three o'clock this afternoon. The man then left—but, at his own suggestion, he left the diamonds with Ehrenfeldt!"

"He did!" said Charlesworth. "That seems——"

"Of course, Ehrenfeldt gave him a receipt for them," continued Mappleson. "But whether it looks very innocent and confiding on the man's part, he did!—and Ehrenfeldt has them. Now, as I told you, Ehrenfeldt knew I was in town—I have had small transactions with him, now and then—and putting together his suspicions and the fact that I had seen the Verringham necklace, he decided to see me. He found out that I was staying here and came to see me last night. He told me the story, and he showed me the diamonds. And now, gentlemen, having told you all this, I am going to tell you still more! In my opinion, those diamonds formed part of the Verringham necklace, and from the description of him given me by Ehrenfeldt I believe the man who is offering them is the late Sir Charles Stanmore's butler—whose name I cannot recollect."

"Bedford!" exclaimed Charlesworth.

"I cannot recollect it. But I saw the man—at close quarters—when I was down there at Aldersyke, on my return from Paris, talking to you gentlemen. Ehrenfeldt described him closely—I am sure he is the man!"

"But—the widow lady?" suggested Charlesworth.

"Pooh!—some catspaw, or woman pressed into service," replied Mappleson. "If my suspicions are correct about the butler, Bedford, of course he'll have accomplices. This is not a one man job!"

"It will require a rather clever woman to impersonate a lady of old family," remarked Gilford. "Unless, indeed, your man Ehrenfeldt is easily taken in."

"I don't think Ehrenfeldt is likely to be taken in by anything," replied Mappleson. "But let us get to business! Ehrenfeldt is coming to see me here, at two o'clock. I want you to be here—all three. I want you to arrange with him that you can be on the spot at his office when these people call, and to fix things so that you can see the man. If he is Bedford, as I suspect, you will no doubt have questions to ask him——"

"About more matters than one!" muttered Charlesworth. "Yes," he continued in louder tones, "and we shall also be interested in seeing the lady. But can Ehrenfeldt manage to stow us away somewhere so that we can observe and not be observed ourselves?"

"I think he will manage that," replied Mappleson. "But come back here a little after two and you will find him with me."

The three men went away, discussing the information they had just received.

"What lies behind all this—if the man is Bedford?" said Gilford. "Something, evidently, took place at Aldersyke Manor on the night of my partner's murder of which we know nothing. But what?"

"If this man is Bedford, let us get hold of him, and we'll soon clear that up, Mr. Gilford!" said Charlesworth. "Bedford is a damned sly chap—that's evident—but he's the sort that will squeal if he's pinched. If Bedford *is* the man, Bedford has had confederates. Mappleson was right—there'll be accomplices. What I'm chiefly anxious about is—who is the lady of family, or, perhaps, who's the woman who's going to impersonate her?"

Gilford considered matters awhile in silence.

"I think," he said at last, "I really think that if Bedford is the man we ought to be very careful. Bedford, I am inclined to believe, might be a very dangerous man to tackle if he were forced into a corner. Those quiet, apparently innocuous sort of men generally are. I think we should adopt very careful tactics indeed!"

"Oh, we'll fix it!" replied Charlesworth. "We're going to be there, anyway. We'll settle it with this man Ehrenfeldt."

But Ehrenfeldt, duly met in company with Mappleson, shortly after two o'clock, had evidently thought out a plan of campaign for himself. He listened to what Charlesworth had to say and then, without comment, introduced his own proposals.

"Yes," he said, "but I do not want any trouble, any scenes, eh, in my own office, you understand? It pays me best to keep out of it as far as I can, eh? So I think what you will do is like this. There is a friend of mine has his office on the ground floor, under mine—I have arranged with him that you can go in there and look through his wire blind into the street. At three o'clock this steward man and the lady will come up to my office—you can inspect them as they arrive. Now it is for me, what I do with them: I have consulted with friend Mappleson here on that point. Well, I talk to them, chiefly to the lady, to find things out, eh? I get all I can out of her and so on and so on. Finally, I tell her I can't do this deal on my own, no! I consult my friends about it—I see what we can do—what offer we can make—and she is to call again to-morrow to hear what I have to say. In the meantime I insist on their taking the diamonds away with them and giving me back my receipt. Then they go, and walk down the stairs—and at the bottom, I think you will be—eh?—waiting for them! It is a good place. I cannot have scenes in my office, you understand."

"It'll do," said Charlesworth. He looked at his watch. "More than half-past two now," he continued. "You'd better take us round, Mr. Ehrenfeldt, and introduce us to your friend on the ground floor."

"Plenty of time, plenty of time," replied Mr. Ehrenfeldt, placidly. "All goes well if you follow my arrangements—we finish our cigars, eh?"

But Charlesworth was impatient to get to work; the mystery about Bedford and the lady of decayed family was urging him to do something, and he whispered to Mappleson to get the diamond merchant away. Mr. Ehrenfeldt eventually complied, but instead of leading his newly-found friends openly along Holborn towards Hatton Garden, he conducted them thither by a devious route which led first through Gray's Inn, across Gray's Inn Road, and by a series of slums beyond Brooke Street. Finally emerging into the street of diamonds at its top end, he suddenly shot them into a narrow entry and without any ceremony into a room on the ground floor, the dirty windows of which were effectually screened from the street by thickly-meshed wire blinds.

There was but one man in this room, a Hebraic gentleman in a coat with a fur collar, who sat at a centre table smoking a very large cigar of strong odour, and showed no surprise at this incursion on his privacy. Mr. Ehrenfeldt waved a hand, first at him, then at his companions.

"Mr. Mosenstein," he said. "The gentlemen that I speak of, Mr. Mosenstein. You let them look through your windows a little, eh?"

"So!" responded Mr. Mosenstein, hospitably. He glanced about him as if in search of something. "I don't have but two chairs in this room," he remarked apologetically. "Perhaps you sit on the table, what?"

"Oh, we're all right, thank you, sir," said Charlesworth. "The window's what we want." He turned to Ehrenfeldt. "Your office is above this?" he asked. "First floor? All right—don't keep them talking too long after they arrive. We'll be in the passage at the foot of the stairs."

"So!" agreed Mr. Ehrenfeldt. He disappeared, and the three watchers disposed themselves at the window while Mr. Mosenstein, watching them, continued to smoke placidly. Ten minutes passed—twenty—then, all of a sudden, a cab drove up and stopped. A man got out; turned his face towards the house; a woman followed him. And Charlesworth spoke, sharply.

"Good God!" he muttered. "Bedford! And—Mrs. John Stanmore!"

CHAPTER XXV
THE OPEN WINDOW

Charlesworth was quick to see that Mrs. John Stanmore was in a state of nervous excitement—or of fear. As Bedford handed her out of the cab she glanced apprehensively at the house, and while he paid and dismissed the driver she looked up and down the street as if suspicious or frightened of her surroundings. As for Bedford, his movements were quick and decisive. Turning from the cabman he directed Mrs. Stanmore's attention to the open door and pointed within to the stair which led to Ehrenfeldt's office on the first floor. Talking with evident rapidity all the time, he then pointed her down the street in the direction of Holborn Viaduct; Mrs. Stanmore, nodding as if in comprehension, turned away and walked slowly in that direction. And Bedford, after watching her for a second, made for the doorway and they heard him running up the stairs. A moment later and a door opened and closed.

"Queer!" muttered Charlesworth. "Why has she gone away? And will she come back?"

"Evident, I think," said Mappleson. "The man wants to have a word or two in private with Ehrenfeldt. But—the man is Bedford, eh?"

"Bedford!—right enough!" replied Charlesworth, with a cynical laugh. "Oh, yes, that's Bedford! Well . . . I think Bedford's trapped! Out of this house he doesn't go without me. Safe, up there, I think. And I suppose the lady will come back presently and go up there, too. But—Mrs. John Stanmore! In league with Bedford! There'll be some strange revelations, Mr. Mappleson!"

He laughed again, and there was a note of chagrin in the laughter—Charlesworth was wondering why the devil he had never harboured any suspicion of these two. Mrs. John Stanmore! Good Heavens!—he had never even thought of *her*! And yet—why, of course, she'd had equal opportunities with any of the other people living at Aldersyke Manor at the time of Sir Charles' death. And after all she was Guy's mother, and if she knew that Guy was about to be cut off with a miserable £500 a year and that she could save his inheritance by sacrificing her brother-in-law, why—there you were! Strange that he'd never thought of that before!—and now to find Bedford in collusion with her—it was a turnover of things that he'd never anticipated. And now he was eager to get to grips with the truth, and he looked excitedly down the street in the hope of seeing Mrs. Stanmore's immediate return and hearing her climb the stairs to Ehrenfeldt's office. . . .

"We'll follow her up there as soon as she comes back," he said, thinking aloud. "Catch both of 'em red-handed, so to speak. I suppose they'll have those diamonds on them——"

The door of Mosenstein's room opened: Ehrenfeldt came in—alone. Charlesworth made for him, hurriedly. Ehrenfeldt nodded.

"All right, all right!" he said. "The lady comes back, soon. Just a moment—I keep the fish playing for you a little while. All right!"

He went up to Mosenstein's table and spoke a few words to him in an undertone, and in a language which neither Charlesworth nor Sherman understood. Mosenstein nodded, got up, and left the room with Ehrenfeldt; Charlesworth, opening the door slightly, saw them go upstairs. He turned to Mappleson.

"Did you understand what Ehrenfeldt said to the other man?" he asked.

"Yes," replied Mappleson. "He asked him to go upstairs for a minute to look at some diamonds. That——"

What Mappleson was going to say further, Charlesworth never knew. There came suddenly from upstairs a shout of alarm, a stampede on the landing, and a wild call from Ehrenfeldt.

"Hi—hi! You come up here—quick, you come! He is gone!"

With an imprecation on his luck, Charlesworth darted out of the door and up the stairs. Ehrenfeldt stood just within his office, pointing excitedly to the window, the lower sash of which was wide open.

"He must have gone through there while I leave him for the moment!" he exclaimed. "Gone!—when Mosenstein and I come up, he is gone—vanish!"

Charlesworth dashed across the room to the open window and looked out. He saw at once how easy it had been for Bedford to get clear away. A few feet below the level of the window was a low building projecting from the outer wall of the house; it was but a drop of a few feet to that; another drop of a few feet to a yard below. Out of that yard a door, now standing ajar, admitted to a narrow passage which ran in the direction of Great Saffron Hill and Farringdon Road: within a couple of minutes of escaping from Ehrenfeldt's office, Bedford would be in the midst of teeming crowds. And

Charlesworth, muttering a hearty curse, turned to Ehrenfeldt.

"Those diamonds?" he exclaimed. "Did he bring them?"

Ehrenfeldt spread his hands, and then pointed to his desk.

"He bring the lot!" he said. "They are there, spread out, when I leave him for a moment, to ask Mosenstein here to come and look at them. He suggest that his own self. 'Let somebody else, who is an expert, see them, too,' he say. 'See them before the lady arrive.' So—I leave him to fetch Mosenstein. Leave the diamonds, too—just there, where I show you. Then, when we come back, Mosenstein and me—gone! Diamonds—and him! Vanish—pouf!"

"Why didn't the lady come in with him?" growled Charlesworth.

"He say he wish to see me alone, first," replied Ehrenfeldt. "She come presently—take a little walk along the street; then come. You find her outside, eh? But as for him—eh, well, it is as I tell you, as you see! Gone! And those diamonds—worth—oh!"

Charlesworth ran down the stairs and into the street. But he saw nothing of Mrs. John Stanmore. And presently he called Sherman outside.

"No use hanging round here!" he said. "Come on, let's get busy after this fellow. As to the woman, I reckon she's off, too! But what on earth did they come here at all for? Here, let's get to the nearest telephone."

"Post-office along there—opposite side," said Sherman. "Telephone there."

Charlesworth crossed the street and hurried along, with Sherman at his heels, and Mappleson, who had followed them out, in close attendance. They had not gone far before they were aware of a crowd gathered at the entrance to a tea-shop opposite the post-office and near the end of the street. Re-crossing, Charlesworth forced his way to the tea-shop door and asked a policeman standing there what was the matter, at the same time showing his card.

"Lady died suddenly, inside," replied the policeman laconically. "Walked in, ordered some tea, and died, they say, while she was drinking it."

Charlesworth pushed into the shop, followed closely by the other two. And he pushed, too, into the midst of a group gathered near a small table in a corner, in the centre of which, still lying in the chair in which she had died, was Mrs. John Stanmore. There was a doctor there, and he was saying just what Charlesworth expected him to say.

"Heart failure—probably been hurrying," said the doctor.

But Charlesworth muttered something to himself and went out—to get on the track of Bedford.

* * * *

If Bedford had not made a little miscalculation of his chances—as nearly all criminals do—he might have got away very easily with the Verringham diamonds and with the considerable amount of cash which they found in his pockets when they searched him. But Bedford forgot something—again, as nearly all criminals do. He forgot, when he climbed out of Ehrenfeldt's window, that that window was overlooked by a great many other windows: if he didn't overlook it, he took great odds against himself. And as a matter of fact, there happened to be looking out of one of those over-looking windows a sharp youth who just then had nothing to do and was so vastly interested in seeing a man climb out of Ehrenfeldt, the diamond merchant's window and sneak away from the yard beneath, that he promptly went after him, and following Bedford into Farringdon Street promptly pointed him out to a sergeant and a constable who happened to stand handy at a street corner and told them what he had seen. And what Bedford had to say was not satisfactory, and the sergeant and constable took him in charge, and when, a little later, they found a quantity of loose diamonds and a lot of bank-notes and other valuables on him, they communicated with Headquarters, and by tea-time Charlesworth and Bedford met again.

* * * *

"He was a queer chap, Bedford," said Charlesworth, talking to a friend a day or two after Bedford had been hanged at Pentonville. "As queer a chap as ever I came across. Of course, plenty came out at the trial, but I knew more than came out there or elsewhere. Bedford sent for me after it was all over and when he knew there wasn't a chance for him, and he told me all about it. The real truth was this. Sir Charles Stanmore, who was another queer character, had certain views for his nephew Guy, and certain views for his daughter Irene—who, until all this came out, never knew she was his daughter. Well, Guy and Irene smashed these views to pieces by getting married secretly. A little time before his death Sir Charles found out about this secret marriage—how he found it out nobody knows, and probably never will know. He was a revengeful devil, Sir Charles!—he immediately began preparing to make these young people suffer. But—and here comes in the most important thing!—the very morning before his death, and after he'd had a row with Irene, he discovered—perhaps from her—that Mrs. John Stanmore knew of the marriage and had kept it from him. So he'd a holy row with her, and before leaving for town, he told her plainly that instead of leaving her £25,000, and Irene £25,000, and Guy the immense revenue, he should cut his legacy to her down to £1,000 and leave Guy and Irene no more than £500 a year each for life, and, moreover, that he should alter his proposed new will to that effect next day. Next day, mind you!—so there wasn't much time to be lost. Now then, what happened? To begin with, Mrs. John went in tears and tribulation to Bedford and told him of Sir Charles' threat, and she moaned and groaned over the pauperism to which she and Guy and Irene were to be reduced. Of course—according to himself—Bedford could do no more than express the pious hope that Sir Charles' hard heart would be softened. Mrs. John, however, appears to have had more faith in practical measures than in sentimental processes. And that night—again according to himself—Bedford and Purser, indulging in a little quiet conversation, somewhere in its vicinity and where they themselves were unseen, saw Mrs. John steal into the butler's pantry, where the supper-tray for Sir Charles was laid out ready for Purser to take into the study. Purser stole after her, and peeped through the crack of the door, and saw Mrs. John, but with her back to Purser, bending over the tray as if inspecting it. Now Mrs. John did a good deal of superintendence, and Purser concluded that she was just seeing that the tray was all right. But next day, when rumours began to circulate as to the causes of Sir Charles' death in the night, Bedford and Purser got hold of Mrs. John and accused her, point-blank, of murdering her brother-in-law! She neither denied nor confessed it, but began to bargain with them. Then Bedford took the situation completely in hand. He agreed with Mrs. John to square Purser, and he made an arrangement with Purser, who was to have a very nice sum per week for life and an occasional bonus into the bargain. Then he accused Mrs. John of having secured the Verringham necklace, and finding that she had it, he forced her to hand it over to him. And, thirdly, recognizing that it might be a very handy thing to have, and before the doctors got hold of the whole bag of tricks, Bedford emptied the contents of one of the bottles in the Borgia Cabinet into a bottle of his own—and took good care of it. It was with that stuff that he impregnated the chocolates that he sent to Purser; it was the same stuff that he used in eventually getting rid of Mrs. John. And now to end with, I'll tell you exactly what Bedford did on that last day of his liberty. He wanted to be off—and with all the wealth he could get together. He'd tried Gilford for the £5,000—principal and interest—which Guy Stanmore owed him; he'd also tried to sell the diamonds to Ehrenfeldt. Gilford wouldn't pay; Ehrenfeldt wouldn't buy except from the principal, the lady of decayed family. So Bedford, having the whip hand of her, turned his attention to Mrs. John Stanmore! First of all that morning, he made her sell out some stock of her own and pay him £5,000 in cash. Then he forced her to accompany him to Ehrenfeldt's in the character of the real owner of the diamonds—but he had no intention of taking her there. He made her lunch with him somewhere in the neighbourhood of Holborn, and he poisoned her, calculating to a nicety when she would expire. When they reached Ehrenfeldt's, he sent her down the street, told her to go into the tea-shop and get a cup of tea, and at the end of half an hour to return to Ehrenfeldt's and walk upstairs. Then, diamonds and money in pocket, he went up to Ehrenfeldt's, made a show of the stones, asked Ehrenfeldt to get another expert to examine them, and as soon as Ehrenfeldt had left the room, pocketed them and went out of the window. A damned cool, calculating chap!—and possessed of a very queer way of looking at things! 'It was a most unfortunate thing for me, Mr. Charlesworth,' he said, in winding up his story, 'a really deplorable thing that that young fellow should attach any importance to my getting out of the window! I had figured on anybody who saw me taking me for a window-cleaner. A great pity, sir, that a little thing like that should spoil a man's future!—I'd intended to do very well, Mr. Charlesworth, when I'd got safely away, I had indeed!' There was an obvious remark that I might have made on that," concluded Charlesworth, "and I was sorely tempted to make it. But I knew Bedford by that time. He was, like most criminals of his sort—diabolically clever to a certain degree, but beyond that a perfect fool!"

Printed in Dunstable, United Kingdom

81178470R00092